CW00926872

THE LAST STRAW
& MORE

HELEN PARKER

By the same author (for younger readers):
Let the Land Breathe, Net Gain

Copyright © Helen Parker 2003
First published 2003
Scripture Union, 207–209 Queensway, Bletchley, Milton Keynes,
MK2 2EB, England.
Email: info@scriptureunion.org.uk
Website: www.scriptureunion.org.uk

ISBN 1 85999 646 9

Scripture quotations are from the Good News Bible published by
The Bible Societies © 1966, 1971, 1976, 1992 American Bible
Society, and from the New International Version, copyright © 1973,
1978, 1984 by International Bible Society. Used by permission of
Hodder & Stoughton, a member of the Hodder Headline Group.
All rights reserved.

British Library Cataloguing-in-Publication Data.
A catalogue record of this book is available from the British
Library.
Printed and bound in Great Britain by Bookmarque Ltd, Croydon,
Surrey.

Cover: Hurlock Design

✍ *Scripture Union is an international Christian charity working with
churches in more than 130 countries, providing resources to bring the
good news about Jesus Christ to children, young people and families
and to encourage them to develop spiritually through the Bible and
prayer.
As well as our network of volunteers, staff and associates who run
holidays, church-based events and school Christian groups, we
produce a wide range of publications and support those who use our
resources through training programmes.*

Contents

For Rachael and Jenny

The last straw

'Mum, don't close the curtains yet. It's only three o'clock!' Arun turned up the gas fire, and patted the armchair next to it to persuade her to sit down. She did, arranging the folds of her sari, and he opened the curtains again. Arun hated it when she shut out the daylight, even if it *was* a dark winter's afternoon.

He noticed she had put her needlework aside. It was usually the one thing she really enjoyed. 'Why don't you do some sewing?' She shook her head and turned away.

'Do you want a cup of tea, Mum? Shall I make one?'

'Yes please, Arun. You're a good boy. I don't know what will become of you, growing up in this godless country. Dark all day. Cold all year. Unfriendly all the time.'

Arun went through to the kitchen, but he could still hear her moaning. The flat was too small to get away from it. He couldn't help arguing back. 'You've been here for nine years, Mum. Surely you've got used to it by now?'

'Nine years, is it? It feels like eternity. But don't you forget I was at home in Allahabad for twenty-eight years before that! I'll never get used to it here.'

'Well, this is *my* home,' Arun said crossly. But he said it so quietly he knew she wouldn't hear. Instead, he banged the tea cup and jug down more noisily than necessary. Arun had only been four when they'd left India. He could hardly remember it at all.

He took the tea in and put it on the small table beside his mother. 'I had no idea it would be like this, Arun,' she said mournfully. 'A Christian country? Huh!'

Arun didn't reply. They'd been over the same ground again and again. She had thought that in Britain, everyone would wear a big smile and say 'God bless you' all the time. She'd thought there'd be no crime, and that all the neighbours would be friendly.

'What I *really* fancy, Arun, is a pakora. Something with a bit of flavour in it. Be a treasure and run down to the corner shop for me, will you?'

Arun gritted his teeth. 'Can't you send Nandita? I went last time,' he complained.

'Your sister's getting ready to go out with her friends.'

'What about Daleep?'

'What *about* Daleep?' said Daleep, appearing the moment Arun said his name.

'Arun's being difficult about going to the corner shop for me,' his mother sighed. 'He's been such a good boy, making tea, and cheering me up. Now he won't...'

'I'm off to the gym. Sorry.' Daleep didn't sound sorry at all.

'OK. I'll come down with you now if you're going out,' said Arun quickly. He breathed a sigh of relief, stuffed his arms into his jacket, and grabbed some change from the mantelpiece.

Daleep slung his sports bag over one shoulder,

and shut the front door of the flat behind them. They ran down the two flights of stairs. At the bottom, The Nails were hanging around, smoking in the entrance. They were the local gang. They liked to think they were really hard. Hard as nails. Andy's hair was green this time, and Arun noticed another piercing in his nose. He and Safraz were leaning against the wall, blowing lazy smoke rings up the stairwell, their eyes half closed. Sasha was sitting on a wheeliebin with Denzil draped around her. Angie and Tazeem were sitting on the bottom stair. Angie was painting her nails which Arun could see were chewed and bitty. She and Tazeem glanced up as Daleep and Arun came down, but didn't move out of the way. Daleep towered above them. Slowly, they turned their heads. Angie and Sasha were only thirteen like Arun, but they liked to make out they were much older.

'Ooh, Daleep! How are you today, Daleep?' Angie got up slowly, making the most of her long legs and very short skirt.

Tazeem looked them both up and down. 'You taking Pimple with you today then, Daleep?'

Daleep ignored the question. The boys watched but didn't say anything. They knew better than to tangle with Daleep. He was eighteen – at least two years older than them, and twice as strong.

'You could come, you know,' Daleep told Arun once they were outside. 'To the gym. Tuesday night is NRG night. For thirteen to sixteens. You can use most of the equipment, and the weights are supervised by experts. Might put some muscle on you.'

'Doubt it,' Arun replied gloomily.

'And there's the boxing club…'

He didn't need to go on. They'd talked about it before. The Nails never gave Daleep any grief even though there were three boys in the gang, and Daleep was on his own. He put it down to having learned boxing. He thought that if Arun went to a boxing club, he wouldn't have any more problems with them either.

Arun had thought about it a lot. But one thing bothered him. Since Daleep had learned boxing, he'd become so hard. Not just tough, but hard. He got angry about everything and everyone. It was as though the flat had become a punch bag. Not that he ever hit anyone. But he got so angry you could have cut the atmosphere with a knife. His dad wouldn't stand for it, so when he and Daleep were in the same room, the rest of the family kept their heads down. Nandita went out all the time, and Arun's mum just cried.

At the corner shop, Arun wandered along the shelves till he found the pakoras, saying 'Hi' to Mr Singh on his way. Mr Singh was busy explaining the cash-till to his new, young employee. The guy didn't look any older than Arun, though he must have been sixteen. But while Mr Singh's back was turned, quick as a flash, a hand reached behind the counter and nicked a packet of cigarettes.

'Hey!' Mr Singh shouted, moving clumsily round the counter to get to the door. But by the time he looked outside, the thief was long gone.

'Did you see who that was, Arun?'

'No, sorry Mr Singh.'

Arun hadn't seen. But even if he had, he wouldn't

have had the courage to admit it. Grassing wasn't very popular where he lived.

He bought the pakoras, and walked slowly back to the entrance to the flats. Outside, he waited as usual across the road, until someone else arrived. Out of sight in a doorway, he watched the world go by... old men with sticks and grubby raincoats... groups of giggling girls in skimpy tops, despite the cold.

Finally, Mrs Lee Fan from the top floor went into the block with her three small kids. Arun shot across the road and reached the stairway at the same time. Mrs Lee Fan turned and smiled when she saw him. 'Oh, Arun! Please to carry Ming Ha up to flat for me.' She dumped the baby in Arun's arms. Ming Ha was sticky and fidgety. No wonder, in all those pink frills, Arun thought to himself. He wondered if his mum had ever dressed Nandita like that.

Meanwhile, The Nails exploded in mocking laughter. Arun sighed. So much for his street cred. Not that he had any. Anyway, he carried Ming Ha all the way to the top of the block, and waited till Mrs Lee arrived with the buggy and the other two children, and got out her key. She folded up the buggy, and took the baby from Arun. 'Thanks, Arun. You good boy.'

'No problem,' Arun sighed, though it wasn't true. He trudged back down to his flat, trying without success to rub the chocolatey goo from the shoulder of his sweatshirt.

'Arun! Where have you been? I finished my tea long ago,' called his mother. 'Now that you've brought the pakoras, I'll need another cup.'

'Hey, Pimple! I'm starving! What food you got?' It was Monday morning, and Andy stood squarely, blocking the bottom of the stairs.

'Haven't got any,' Arun lied. 'Got to get the school bus.' He tried to push past Andy, but Andy held his arm in an iron grasp while Safraz pulled his school bag off his back and opened it, breaking one of the buckles.

'Smokey bacon! My favourite!' Safraz said, taking out a bag of crisps. 'And a chocolate biscuit.'

'What about *real* food?' Andy objected. 'Ain't 'e got no pie or rolls or nothin'?'

'Wait a minute!' Safraz emptied Arun's school books on to the floor, and dug his onion samosas out of the bag. 'And a can of Coke! And what's this? An apple? Don't need none of this rabbit stuff.' He dropped the apple on to the concrete floor and crushed it with his boot.

'Thanks, Arun. You good boy,' said Safraz, mimicking Mrs Lee Fan's voice and Chinese accent. They lolled against the wall, eating the samosas and crisps, leaving Arun to gather up his school books and run for the bus.

Arun was late for school, so Mr Nevis gave him an instant detention. It wasn't Ben Nevis's fault, thought Arun. He was a decent guy really, a popular teacher. He taught history, but he was also their class tutor so they saw him every morning. But rules were rules, and Arun wasn't going to go squealing about Andy and Safraz and his packed lunch.

The first lesson was FCT – Food and Consumer Technology. It wasn't Arun's best subject. In fact, most of the boys in his class hated it. Mrs Elliot was tall and bony, with a witch's hooked nose. She looked a hundred years old but she still had lots of energy and a football field voice. Arun was sure she was teaching when girls learned cookery and boys did woodwork and swapping over was unheard of. She just seemed to disapprove of boys because they were boys. Many of the girls hated FCT, too.

Mrs Elliot put everyone into pairs. She put Arun with Jessica. Jessica was about twice as tall as Arun, and three times as heavy. When Jessica walked down the corridor, a space cleared for her. She'd been as big as a woman since the beginning of high school. They were all in awe of her mother, too. Jessica's mother spoke with a Jamaican accent even though she had been brought up in Scotland. And Jessica had the same voice – rich and deep. She didn't say much, but when she did speak everyone listened.

The other thing about Jessica was that she fought. And she always won. She didn't fight the girls. That was beneath her dignity. She fought the boys, and they didn't refuse to fight because they didn't want to look stupid. She had even flattened boys three years older than her. Mind you, thought Arun, she hadn't been in so much trouble recently. Maybe she was growing out of it. But having to work with Jessica didn't help Arun's enthusiasm for FCT.

The recipe of the day was sponge cake. Mrs Elliot went on and on about how it had to be light as a feather – a whiff of fresh air. That brought a grunt and a snort from Jessica, and a few giggles from a group of kids behind them who couldn't imagine a whiff being fresh.

They were halfway through the lesson when Phil

Dakers, at the table next to them, said there was no flour left in the plastic flour box. He looked around for Mrs Elliot. 'She's gone to look in on the lower sixth. They're settin' up for an assessment,' Jessica told him, 'but she keeps flour on the top shelf of the store cupboard.'

Phil opened the store cupboard door. It was stacked with food in enormous packets, jars, tins, bags and pots. On the top shelf there were bags of flour. Inside the cupboard, behind the door, was a small step ladder about a metre high – the sort shopkeepers used to reach the high shelves. But one hinge was wobbly.

'The step's broken,' Phil observed. 'Here, Arun! Hold it for me!'

'OK,' said Arun, squatting down to hold the step firmly while Phil stood on it.

'Oof! It's heavy!' Phil grunted, heaving at the bag and trying to brace himself against a lower shelf. Arun tightened his grip.

Then it happened. The flour bag dislodged, and Phil lost his balance. He jumped off and stepped back, and Arun let go of the steps and ducked as the flour bag fell with a whoomph on to the step ladder, splitting open and spilling its contents like a nuclear mushroom cloud all over the store cupboard, and especially over Arun. He closed his eyes tight and coughed a bit. For a second there was an eerie silence, then the whole class broke out into shouts and cheers and whoops of joy.

Arun stood up slowly. His black trousers and school sweatshirt were white from top to toe. He shook his head gently and showers of flour drifted softly to the floor. He moved out of the store cupboard to stand in the classroom, leaving a thick trail of flour wherever he walked. Phil patted his back and choked on the clouds of flour which puffed out of him. The whole class clapped and roared with laughter. Claire, Holly, Karen and Gemma were grinning and clapping. They formed a line and started to chant like cheer leaders, 'Way to go, Arun! Way to go, Arun!' Arun turned around slowly, then did a theatrical bow.

He was really enjoying himself, but it was too good to last. The racket brought Mrs Elliot storming back into the classroom, her wrinkly face red with anger. 'Arun Banerji! Whatever...?! How dare you go into my store cupboard? How could you...! I don't know what...!' It was the first time she had ever been completely stuck for words. An immediate hush had fallen over the rest of the class, and they sidled unobtrusively back to their tables.

'Sorry, Mrs Elliot,' Arun muttered. 'I didn't mean to... I was just trying to...'

'It wasn't his fault, Mrs Elliot,' Phil began. 'I ran out of—'

'No one asked your opinion, Philip Dakers!' she spat out. 'When I wish to hear from you, I will say so!' She looked around at the mess, and suddenly Arun realised it was going to take quite some clearing up. The colour had drained from her face.

'Go outside, Arun. Right outside. Take the side door out on to the netball court, and brush as much of that flour off yourself as you can. Then find a wash basin and wash your hands and face. Then come back at lunchtime, *and* after school if necessary, and clean this room until it's as good as *I* left it.'

Arun shuffled to the classroom door and closed it behind him, sending clouds of flour into the air. He stood still for a moment and coughed some more. Arun thought how his mum would grumble. She liked to wash his school uniform at the weekend, not during the week. And if he had to stay after school, he'd miss the bus, again. And it wasn't his fault.

Trying to drop as little flour as possible, Arun walked down the corridor slowly and stiffly. Two boys overtook him. He recognised them vaguely. They were younger than him, but the same size. It doesn't do anything for your self-respect, being nearly fourteen and only as tall as an eleven-year-old, thought Arun. They sniggered as they looked him up and down. 'It's Arun Banerji,' hissed one. 'He looks like the abominable snowman.'

'Nah,' the other disagreed. 'Too dark for a snowman. Just abominable!' They both giggled.

Something inside Arun exploded. He pounced on the one who'd said he was too dark, got him in a headlock and forced him to the floor. Sitting astride him, Arun rained down punches on his chest until the other boy tried to pull him off. Flinging out his fist, Arun caught the boy full in the face, and he fell back against the wall, moaning. The boy underneath Arun caught him by the hair and Arun thumped him on the nose.

Arun's class must have heard the commotion. Phil Dakers and Shack Robertson came out of the FCT classroom and pulled Arun off the boy, pinning his arms behind him. Arun felt tremendously satisfied as he noticed both boys had bleeding noses.

Sitting outside the head teacher's study 'to cool down and think about it,' Arun lost the warm glow of satisfaction, and just felt fed up. He was still covered in flour, had a split lip and a few bruises, no packed lunch to look forward to, and had to stay behind after school. He sniffed and swallowed hard.

Suddenly, Jessica came and flopped down on a chair beside him. Arun guessed that wasn't unusual. She'd spent a lot of her school hours cooling down in that corridor. He concentrated on ignoring her.

After a minute or two, he could feel her looking at him. His neck and ears began to burn with embarrassment.

'OK,' she said, finally, in her rich, theatrical voice. 'So let me guess how many things have made you mad this mornin'. Six.'

'What?' Arun asked, dazed.

'Number one: your mum's depressed, and she takes it out on you. Two: your dad works all the hours God sends at a job he don' like, and you never see him. Three: you're different from your brother, but he thinks you should be the same, and like the same things as him. Four: The Nails ripped up your homework and made you miss the bus so you got a detention. Five: the flour wasn't your fault, but Smelly Elliot wouldn't listen. An' six: one of them pint-sized white shrimps made a racist comment.'

Arun gaped at her like a fish. The ghost of a smile crossed her face, but soon disappeared.

'How did you know about The Nails?' Arun gasped. She'd got it wrong about the homework... this time. But all the rest was right. In fact, she'd analysed it far more accurately than Arun could ever have done.

'My sister's got a part-time job at the Leisure Centre. She knows Daleep. In fact, she likes Daleep.'

'Yeah,' Arun muttered. 'Most girls do.' But he realised something. If Daleep had told someone about The Nails, he must have noticed. He must know they gave Arun grief.

'He thinks if you took up boxin', like him, you wouldn't have so much trouble with them.'

'Yeah.'

'He cares about his li'l bruvver!' She grinned, and Arun grinned too. 'But you're not really the boxin' type.'

'Right.'

'Take your sweater off.'

'What?'

'Take your sweater off,' she repeated, 'an' I'll take it outside and shake it.'

Arun did so, and when she returned with it, it was just a shade of dark grey instead of snowy white. Arun was glad he hadn't been inside it when she had shaken it.

'Now, go to the bog and do the same with your trousers. And bathe your lip while you're there.'

'What if the head comes?'

'I'll say you were caught short.' She flashed a brilliant white smile, and it lit up her whole face. Arun smiled back, and went off to the toilet.

When he returned with his less white trousers, and with a soothing wet paper towel for his lip, he asked her, 'What are you doing here anyway?'

'Ben Nevis sent me to see how you're doin'.'

'Mr Nevis? Why?'

'We had history next, and Mr Nevis says, "What's up, Jess?" He's a mind reader, that man. So I told him. I didn't say nothin' to Smelly Elliot because she don' listen. But Ben Nevis does. He's fair. He listened, then he told me to come and see how you're gettin' on.'

'But why you?'

'I guess he knew you'd be feeling mad, and he reckons I know what that feels like.' It was her turn to blush. It gave her skin a lovely rich glow, even on a winter's day.

'But you... I mean you're always... it's just that...' Arun got stuck.

She laughed. 'I know. You'd think I was the last person to help anyone cool down. But I'm gettin' better. I don't let my anger get on top of me so much now. Haven't you noticed?'

Arun had. She hadn't been in trouble for fighting for quite a while. But he said, 'I never realised I felt so angry. It took me by surprise.'

'I know,' she nodded. 'It kinda creeps up on you, don' it?'

'And actually,' Arun had to admit, 'those stupid kids weren't making *real* racist remarks.' Arun told her what they'd said – 'Too dark for an abominable snowman. Just abominable!' – and they both laughed.

'I've had far worse,' Arun continued, not laughing any more. 'It was just like the last straw. They lit the fuse, and I went off!'

'I know,' she said again.

They sat in silence for a minute or two. Arun felt a bit better now he could recognise his own feelings.

Finally he asked, 'So what used to make you angry?'

'Oh, everythin'.'

'Racism?'

'Sometimes. But people always seemed to pick on us. Me and my family. One day, my mum came into school. She was wearin' a dress my uncle bought her in Jamaica. Lovely and colourful, it was. Not like the drab stuff you get here. It had pictures of fruit all over it. Someone said, 'Your mum's like a fruit salad,' and someone else goes, 'More like a fruit *cake*. Nutty!' So I jumped on him.'

Arun remembered the incident. The boy was in their year, same height as Jessica, but half the width. It had been no contest.

'Mind you,' she added, 'it was hardly ever one thing in a day. It was the fourth or fifth used to trigger me off. Mostly about my size. It ain't my fault I'm big. So I used to think, 'OK. So I'm big. I might as well make use of it.' She ran her fingers thoughtfully through her carefully plaited hair. Arun noticed that her finger nails were elegantly filed and varnished.

He thought about what she had said. Then suddenly he laughed because it seemed ridiculous that Jessica and he, so totally different, could feel so similar.

She looked at him and grinned. Then she said, 'It's probably you that's as nutty as a fruit cake!'

Arun laughed again, but it hurt his lip, so he stopped. Then he asked, 'So, how is it you don't get into trouble so much these days?'

'Well,' she began. She blushed, and took a deep breath. 'I read to this lady. Every day, on the way home from school. She's blind. Goes to our church. She wanted someone to read the Bible to her. She's white, but it don' make no difference. She's got this little booklet – tells you which bit of the Bible to read each day, and then you get a little comment about the passage. She likes me to read that, too. Sometimes she gives me a bit of pocket money.'

'Yeah?' Arun said, wondering where all this was leading.

'Well,' she went on, 'There's this bit in the Bible. It says, "Don' be so angry that you sin", and "Don' go to bed angry". The booklet said there's nothin' wrong with feelin' angry sometimes. It's OK. You just shouldn't let it make you do bad things. So whenever I felt absolutely spittin', I tried to stop and think what was makin' me mad. And I thought, it's OK to be mad about that. Bet Jesus feels mad about that too. Him and me both. But when Jesus was down here on earth, he didn't never punch nobody on the nose. Know what I mean?'

Arun did. He nodded.

'And sometimes I used to get so mad, I couldn't sleep. I used to plot how I was goin' to get even. But now, I says to myself at bedtime, 'it's OK, Jessica, girl. Jesus knows how you feel. He most likely feels the same.' Then I can go to sleep. No problem.'

It was the longest speech Arun had ever heard Jessica make. She used to be all fists instead of words.

'The Bible's not old and fusty you know,' she said. Arun thought she was afraid he might laugh at her. But first, no one laughed at Jessica. And second, Arun knew the Bible was up-to-date. His mum read it every day.

'It tells you how to live. Now. Even here.' The lunch bell went. 'Want a cheese roll?' Jessica said, opening her school bag. 'My mum packs my lunch. She always gives me too much. Fat lot of good me tryin' to go on a diet.'

She pulled a big packet out of her bag, and handed Arun a roll. 'Eat it quick before the head comes!'

Arun didn't need telling twice.

The race

Phil took the envelope out of his pocket. If no one had been looking, he'd have sealed it with a kiss. It read:

> To: Ella
> Please come to the Athletics Club Valentine Disco
> When? Saturday 14th February, 8 until late
> Where? Granton Athletics Club, Newton Lane
> From: Phil Dakers

The invitation card was printed. Each of the club members had been given one. Phil had just put in the names. He'd done his best handwriting.

He had planned to drop the envelope on to Ella's desk and go straight to his seat, but as he put it down, he stopped dead. She had another identical invitation. She opened his, and laid them side by side. The other one was from Greg Robertson. All the girls followed him around. They called him 'Shack', after the American basketball player, Shaquille O'Neill.

'Now I have a problem, don't I?' Ella smiled. 'Aren't I the lucky one? How am I going to choose between the two favourites to win the Valentine Cross-country Race?'

'Um...' Phil began, but Mr Nevis came in, so he had to go to his seat. He spent the lesson thinking about all the clever answers he *could* have given her, like 'Choose the better-looking guy, after all,

I've chosen the best-looking girl', or 'No contest!'.
But he'd been too slow.

Then he started writing rhymes:

My thoughts and words are kinda slow,
But watch my feet like lightning go!
Choose the guy whose feet are fast
He's the one whose love will last.
Don't choose Shack, the guy's a fool,
Look around. Choose Phil the Cool!

Now he was really getting into it. The next thing he
knew, Mr Nevis was looking over his shoulder.
Horrified, he tried to lean across his paper, but again
he was too late. He closed his eyes and hunched his
shoulders.

'Hmm! A budding poet, eh, Dakers? The school
magazine needs some bards. I'll keep this for the
Valentine issue.' Phil could feel his face and neck
burning, and he knew he was blushing hard. He was
doubly sure when the kids around him sniggered.

'Whose the lucky bird then, Dakers?' hissed the
boy next to him.

'A bird for the bard!'

'Some skirt for the flirt!'

But in the midst of all the amusement he was
causing, the idea came to him. *Ella* should choose the
winner! That was it! She should go to the Athletics
Club disco with the winner of the cross-country race!
It was a brainwave. He felt pretty confident of
winning, but this was the incentive he needed for all
that extra training.

At the end of the lesson he dropped another note

on Ella's desk. 'Choose the winner of the race!'

She looked up and smiled at him slowly and thoughtfully. 'OK,' she mouthed as he left the classroom.

At the next training session, Shack was showing off as usual, goofing around and roaring with laughter. His white teeth gleamed like a toothpaste advert. Once they'd changed into their kit, he suggested, 'Three times around the track for a warm-up then, Mac?'

Doug Macdonald grinned good-naturedly. 'Three times? That'd be me for the evening, Robertson!' Doug enjoyed running, but he never expected to win. Everyone knew he wanted to become a mathematician, but he claimed he wanted to be 'a fit mathematician'! 'Pick on someone your own size,' he advised Shack. 'How about Phil Dakers? He'd be fair game for you!'

'Spot on, but not yet!' Shack replied. 'I'm gonna save that pleasure for the Valentine Cross-country.' Then he added mysteriously, 'There's other things depending on it.'

Just then Tim, their coach, came in with a young trainee. 'Hi, everyone. This is Daleep. He wants to become a personal trainer, and he's on placement here with us for a month.'

Daleep nodded to everyone. Phil recognised him. He knew he was Arun's big brother, though they were totally different.

'OK now,' Tim continued. 'Everybody done their stretches? Follow me. Let's do some high-knee jogging to begin with.' He led them out on to the track, and they copied his warm-up exercises until everyone was breathing heavily.

It was a good training session. After warming up, Phil and two of the other cross-country runners set off on part of the track to be used for the competition. They agreed to stay together, but normally Phil would have enjoyed the solitude of running on his own. When he was out in the fields and running along the lanes, he felt at peace with himself and everything else. It was easy to concentrate on his pace and rhythm, to think clearly about his tactics, and even to glance at his watch. You couldn't do that with track running. Too many people. Too much noise and hassle. At the end of the session, Phil wasn't even tired. Adrenalin was flowing, and he began to think of Ella as his prize.

Tuesday night was NRG night at the Pulse Centre, when thirteen to sixteen-year-olds were allowed. Phil began on one of the exercise bikes. He'd already worked out a personal fitness programme with one of the regular staff. At each visit he increased his speed and the distance covered.

Phil knew most of the regular faces, but this time there was a boy he didn't recognise. He looked a bit younger than Phil – just thirteen, maybe. He was pedalling the exercise bike as though his life depended on it. He was small but wiry – no fat, all muscle. His face was grim – set to win. He was gritting his teeth in spite of a train-tracks brace. As he pedalled, his ginger hair began to stick to his forehead. His face got redder, and his freckles joined up.

'Steady on,' Phil grinned. 'Don't give it all you've got straight away. Keep a bit in reserve.'

The boy scowled at him. 'Who said you were the expert, then?' he challenged Phil.

'No one! No, I'm not an expert. I just want to get fit – like you. At least, that's what I thought you wanted.'

'So, how does that give you the right to tell me what to do?' the boy growled.

'OK, OK. No offence, pal. It's just that I haven't noticed you here before.' Phil didn't want to pick a fight, or use up his energy arguing. He moved quickly on to the cross-trainer and pedalled the foot-plates forward for two minutes and backward for two, forwards and backwards, feeling his thigh and calf muscles responding, and thinking of Ella to spur himself on. But he kept glancing at the boy. There was something different about him – a gentle kid, trying to act tough.

Phil began to get up half an hour earlier each morning to run before school. It was still dark, and the air was crisp and cold. With just a month to go before the big race and the disco, he wanted to give himself the best chance he could. After his run, he just had time for a shower and a huge bowl of cereal before school. One morning, as he wheeled his bike in at the school gate, he saw Shack leaning against the fence smoking with a group of boys from his class. 'Hey, Dakers!' one of the boys sneered. 'How do you know she's gonna choose *you*? She might choose Romeo, here!'

'She's going to the disco with the winner!'

Phil grinned. 'And may the fittest man win!' he added, promising himself he wouldn't smoke because he didn't want to lessen his lung capacity. There was some jeering and sniggering behind him as he wheeled his bike away from them, but he wasn't worried. Shack was OK really, and he could have been a very good athlete. He was a bit bigger, and probably stronger, but Phil knew it was fitness that counted. And he knew he was fitter than Shack.

Ella was at the classroom door as he arrived. 'All right?' he greeted her. She smiled. The two of them had always been friendly, ever since primary school. They'd been in the same maths set last year, and now they were in the same practical group for chemistry. But it was just recently that Phil had noticed how pretty she was, and how warmly she smiled at him. His determination to win moved up one more place.

The Ginger Fighter was at the Pulse Centre again the following Tuesday. Phil said 'Hi' as he walked past to the treadmill.

Half-way through his programme Phil paused for a swig of water, and the boy paused, too. 'Are you training for something special?' he asked Phil.

'Yeah! Cross-country race. It's on 14th February.'

'Less than two weeks to go, then?' the boy observed.

'Yep. I'm running every day now, training here every week, and down at the Athletics Club Wednesdays and Fridays. How about you?'

'Oh, just want to be fitter,' the boy replied vaguely.

'What's your name? Er… I'm Phil Dakers.'

'Jamie,' said the boy reluctantly, not giving away his surname. 'I must get back to work.' The two boys did some serious training, but before he left the centre Jamie said, 'See you next week?'

'OK,' Phil replied.

At the Athletics Club the pressure was on, and the pace was hotting up. Phil was very hopeful of a medal this time because he was at the top of the age range. Next year he'd be competing against sixteen-year-olds. Of course, he knew his own club members, and he knew some members of the club they'd be racing against – Meadow Beach – some of the lads went to his school. He'd sized up the opposition, and thought he was in with a chance.

On the last Tuesday evening at the Pulse Centre he had planned to give it all he'd got. The following Tuesday would be three days *after* the race, and he was going to stay in with pizza and a video – and, he hoped, with Ella. So he had to reach his peak of fitness this week. It was now or never.

Half-way through his programme he noticed Jamie arriving, head down, trying to hide a hugely swollen black eye.

'Crumbs!' Phil exclaimed. 'What happened to the other guy?'

'None of your business!' Jamie snapped, his old aggression returning. But he went very red, and despite his brave front, Phil had the feeling fighting wasn't Jamie's usual style.

'Er… are you training to be strong enough to

stand up to someone?'

'What are you – psychic or something?' Jamie sniffed.

'Who *is* this guy?' Phil asked quietly. 'What has he got on *you*?'

Jamie wiped his face on his T-shirt. 'I don't know his name. But he's got it in for me because his dad used to work with my dad, at Buckstone Printers, but my dad made him redundant. He wasn't the only one. My dad had to lose thirty people. He hated doing it. But the firm just isn't getting enough orders. It broke my dad's heart. He didn't sleep for ages.'

A flicker of memory crossed Phil's mind. 'What's your dad's name?'

Jamie sighed. 'Fitzpatrick. Alan Fitzpatrick.'

'And does he look like you?' Phil squinted his eyes and tried to imagine a forty-year-old version of Jamie.

'Yeah – only bigger!' Jamie grinned at last.

'I remember! His picture was in the local paper. And there were some words behind him – a poster, wasn't it? Something about justice?'

'Yeah.'

'Wait a minute! It's coming back to me now. "His son's artwork." Did *you* do the poster?'

'Yes.' Jamie blushed, but he went on, 'It was a banner. I made it at church: "God has told us what is right: see that justice is done, and see that mercy is your first concern." It's a verse from the Bible. Dad liked it so much he said it would be his motto at work, so he put it on the wall above his desk.'

'The press made a big thing of it, then?'

'You bet. The headline was "Rough justice from

Buckstone boss." But Dad did his best. He got a good redundancy package for all the people who lost their jobs. I guess it just wasn't enough.'

'Didn't seem much like justice to them, I suppose,' Phil murmured. 'So how does this boy know you? Same school?'

'No. I expect he picked me out because of my dad's photo.'

'What does your dad say about all of this?'

'I haven't told him. It's not his fault.'

'But what about your black eye?'

'He thinks I fell off my bike. Actually, I did but I got this…' He pointed to a grazed knee. 'Not this!' He fingered his black eye gently. Phil wondered about the deception, but he respected Jamie for not whingeing.

'So what does he look like, this guy who's after you?' Phil asked.

'He's strong with curly black hair and big teeth. I think he's a distance runner like you, only he's a bit overweight. I figured that if I trained hard I might be able to outrun him over a sprint distance.' He fingered his black eye again and added, 'I don't think there'd be any point squaring up to him a second time.'

'So he's taking it out on you, for what your dad did to his dad,' Phil repeated slowly, trying to get it right.

'Yes. He knows my name, and my dad's, of course, but he won't tell me his. He threatened Treacle – my dog.' Jamie's chin trembled again. 'Treacle could easily outrun him – it's just me.'

'Is Treacle a big dog?' Phil asked suddenly. 'Why don't you set him on this bully?'

'Yes, he's big. He's a black Labrador. But he's a softy. A big pudding. Treacle pudding! Wouldn't hurt a fly. Anyway, I've got nothing against the guy. I just wish he didn't have so much against *me*!'

Phil thought for a moment, then he said, 'Um, do you go to a youth club or anything? Our church has a great club, called Resolution. You can come if you like. It's for kids of twelve and over. Fridays, seven-thirty to nine-thirty.'

'Er, thanks. I'll think about it.'

One of the Pulse Centre staff sauntered up to them. 'This isn't a chat show, lads. You've paid to use the equipment, you know. I should get to it if I were you.'

'Yeah, sorry,' Phil said.

'No, *I'm* sorry,' Jamie insisted. 'Anyway, good luck for the race!'

Saturday dawned still and dull, a perfect day for running. Phil's race was to begin at three o'clock. He arrived early, looking around eagerly for Ella. She was there in the crowd, in a bright yellow fleece. She smiled at Phil, and gave him a thumbs-up.

By two-fifty the competitors were all signed in and warmed up. Phil jogged gently on the spot. Gradually, the people milling around him began to fade into the background as he prepared mentally for the distance. He was imagining each area of the course, going over it in his mind, when someone clapped him on the back, taking his breath away. 'Watcha, Dakers. Prepare to be a gooseberry tonight!' It was Shack, swigging from a can of fizzy juice. Phil tried to ignore him, but his concentration was shattered, with only minutes to go.

Shack threw his can on to the grass and burped loudly. 'See yer later, babe!' he shouted to Ella. Phil craned his neck. He couldn't see her. People were in the way.

They were under starter's orders. 'On your marks…'

Phil leaned forward, his concentration in shreds. The pistol sounded. They were off. After some elbow jostling, Phil found himself among the first half dozen. Shack was out in front, but Phil wasn't worried. It was very rare for the pace-setter to win. As they pulled away, he began to feel better, as if he was running alone. He could relax and think straight. He stretched out his pace as he entered the woods. His rhythm was going well. He increased his speed, and didn't feel tired. He could go on all day. He expected to catch up with the boy in front of him at the next curve, where the path ran alongside the road.

There was a sudden commotion up ahead – shouting and yelling. His heart missed a beat, and he almost stumbled. As he rounded the bend, he saw a black shape in the bushes, and a figure kneeling beside it. Phil's breathing became ragged, and he lost his rhythm. He recognised the figure.

Jamie.

For a split second, Phil wavered. Ella's pretty face flashed across his mind. If he slowed down now… it wasn't fair! It was *unjust*! But he knew what he had to do.

He stopped and sank to his knees beside the dog. 'What happened?' he panted. Jamie looked round at him, and his mouth dropped open in amazement.

'What're you...? The race! This is your race! But you mustn't stop!'

'What happened?' Phil insisted. The dog was whimpering and scrabbling with three paws, trying to get up. The fourth leg stuck out at a funny angle.

'It was him,' Jamie gasped. 'That big kid. He was running as well. He kicked Treacle. Hurt his leg. I was just taking him for a walk. Didn't know this was part of the track. Didn't mean to get in the way. Anyway, Treacle got him. Bit his hand. It's all right, boy,' he sniffed, hugging the dog. 'Wish I had my mobile with me,' he said to Phil. 'He needs a vet. What can we do?'

'Can we carry him to the road? Maybe someone will stop and help us. Take your jacket off. We could use it as a stretcher.'

Gently, they slid the big dog on to Jamie's coat, and tried to lift him. He was *very* heavy. Runners were passing them now. Some ignored them. Others looked surprised, but no one spoke. They needed all their breath for the race.

Twenty metres further on, the path drew alongside a country road. An old car ground to a halt beside them. A woman looked out anxiously from the passenger seat. Phil recognised her.

'It's Mrs Macdonald!' he exclaimed. 'She must've come to watch Doug in the race.' She was winding down the window to lean out. At the same time a big man leapt out of the driver's seat and strode towards them.

'What have we got here?' he asked kindly, kneeling beside Treacle.

'My dog's hurt. I think his leg might be broken,' Jamie replied.

'Best get him to a vet fast then. I think there's one in Newton High Street. Let's put him in my car. OK?'

'Yes. Er... thanks,' Jamie agreed.

The man was strong, and he picked up Treacle gently and easily. 'What's up, Phil?' asked Mrs Macdonald, anxiously. 'Aren't you running in this race? What happened?'

'I was, but my friend's dog's hurt.'

Mrs Macdonald leaned round. 'This is Tom Robertson, Phil – Greg's dad. We live in the same road. We were hoping to watch the finish of the race.' Phil and Jamie slid on to the back seat beside Treacle. Phil thought it was weird to hear Shack being called 'Greg', his real name.

'OK, lads?' Mr Robertson asked, starting the engine.

Phil stared at Greg's dad in amazement. Father and son *looked* alike, but there the similarity ended. Greg's dad was kind, and he'd handled Treacle so gently.

'Greg's got big hopes for this race,' Mr Robertson said, turning to Mrs Macdonald. 'Says there's a very special prize if he wins.' He drove carefully to the village, trying to avoid the bumps. 'I really hope he gets it,' he added. 'He's had a tough time. When I lost my job, he took it really hard. Tried to stick up for me. It was my fault. I put the whole family in the doldrums for a bit. Couldn't see the light at the end of the tunnel.' Mrs Macdonald was nodding sympathetically.

Phil had the spark of an idea. He glanced at Jamie.

Jamie nodded back, his eyes wide.

'Then I realised that every cloud has a silver lining,' Mr Robertson continued. 'Like, I'm free to come and watch my boy win this race!' He grinned, and his teeth sparkled white. 'Here we are.' He pulled on to the vet's forecourt.

'Er – which company did you work for?' Phil asked, trying to sound casual.

'Buckstone Printers,' Mr Robertson replied.

Everything began to fit together in Phil's mind like a jigsaw puzzle.

Mr Robertson turned back to Mrs Macdonald. 'I was really angry at first. Greg thought it was a racist thing. But there were other guys in the same position – some white, some black. Besides, my boss was a decent guy – no way a racist. He had this thing about trying to do what was right. Everyone respected him. The company just couldn't keep us all.' Phil stole a glance at Jamie, and found him grinning with pride.

They got out of the car, and Phil opened the door to the vet's. Mr Robertson went ahead with Treacle.

'It's him,' Jamie hissed.

'You never told me the boy was black!' Phil whispered.

'Oh! Didn't I? But it doesn't…'

That figures, Phil thought. Alan Fitzpatrick isn't a racist. Neither is Jamie.

'Anyway, I've got good news for Greg,' Mr Robertson finished as he laid Treacle down beside the reception desk. 'I've got a job interview on Monday! If he wins the race, and I get the job, we'll be on cloud nine!' He stood by while Jamie checked Treacle in and phoned his dad.

'Thanks a lot Mr Robertson,' Jamie said finally. 'My dad's coming straight over. You'd better go, or you'll miss the end of the race.' He turned to Phil, 'Sorry, Phil, you missed the race. Thanks for helping me and Treacle. Wonder what the special prize was?'

'It's OK,' Phil muttered.

'Come on, lad,' Mr Robertson urged Phil. 'Let's see if we can get back in time.' Phil climbed into the car. 'Anyway, how did the dog get hurt?'

Phil felt awkward. He didn't know what to say. Jamie had kept quiet, so maybe he should, too. 'Er, I didn't see…'

'Our Greg – he's terrified of dogs. I keep telling him it's daft – great big lad like him, but he can't help it. He was attacked by a big, black dog when he was tiny. Can't seem to forget it.'

Phil's mind was racing, but they'd arrived. Mr Robertson parked the car and they all leapt out. The first dozen runners had finished. Hundreds of people were milling around. Phil looked round frantically for Ella's bright yellow fleece. He spotted her and ran up.

'There you are!' she gasped, grabbing his arm. 'What happened? When you weren't among the first ten, I thought…'

'Who won?'

'Some guy called Andrew something.'

'Not Shack?'

'No. Shack was doing well, but Andrew passed him about 50 metres before the end, then Shack fell and twisted his ankle. But where were you?'

'There was this kid. I knew him from the Pulse Centre. His dog had a broken leg. Big dog. Heavy. So

I stopped to help him.'

'Oh Phil! You're a hero!' Ella said, reaching up to give him a quick peck on the cheek.

Phil felt himself blush. 'But what about the disco?'

'If I can't go with the winner, I'll settle for a hero!'

Phil put his arm around her shoulders. 'But it's a pity for Shack,' she added. 'He won't be going to the disco at all if he's really hurt his ankle.'

They went to where Shack was sitting with a small crowd gathered around him, including his dad.

'Oh no! He's hurt his hand as well!' Ella exclaimed. Phil saw that Shack's hand was bleeding.

'But that's because...' 'Phil began. Then he stopped. Shack hadn't had much going for him recently. Maybe this was the moment for mercy, rather than justice.

Instead, he looked at Ella. She's not just a pretty face, he thought. She's got a kind heart as well. And she's going to the disco with ME!

Fiddling

Claire's mum swung the car into the shopping centre car park, past the church where there was always a big chart showing how much money had been raised for repairs to the huge roof. A Bible text was printed beside it: 'God loves a cheerful giver'. Claire snorted, and sank further down in her seat. She didn't think she'd ever be a cheerful giver, or a cheerful *anything*, for that matter.

'What's up now?' Alison asked. Alison, the sickeningly perfect younger sister. Miss Slim-and-Blonde, neat and pretty, polite and pleasant, and very good at French. Sucker!

'Oh, do try and cheer up, love,' Mum pleaded. 'We only go shopping once a week.'

'Can I look round the shops while you and Alison do the supermarket stuff, Mum? Can I? Please?'

Mum sighed. Claire knew that if she said yes, it would probably be because she knew Claire would make life difficult in the supermarket. She always did. 'Oh, I suppose so, love,' Mum agreed reluctantly.

It didn't make Claire feel any better. Worse, if anything. More guilty. Less cheerful.

'Meet us back at the car in, er, forty minutes then? OK?'

It wasn't as if she wanted to be awkward or grumpy. It just happened. It was something to do with Saturdays. Saturdays were supposed to be fun.

No school. Chance to do all those fabulous things the people on CBBC got up to on Saturday mornings. Like Holly and her brother, Martin, who always went to the dry-ski slope on Saturdays, practising for real snow in the Scottish Highlands. In your dreams, Claire told herself miserably.

She sat on the low ornamental wall, and stared angrily at the neat, orderly pots of pink flowers. 'Keep Newtown tidy!' dictated the sign above the garden.

Why? thought Claire illogically, and felt ridiculously pleased to see cigarette ends in the plant pots.

She transferred her gaze to the feet of the passers-by. There were clicky heels and suede Hush Puppies, heavy Doc Marten's and Clarks' sandals. Mostly, there were trainers. Someone was wearing the same trainers as her. She looked up with momentary interest, but instantly wished she hadn't. The wearer was a greasy-haired, spotty boy, about her own age, with a brace on his teeth. He stared at her. She looked down and picked her nails intently.

Most girls her age were in twos or threes, or in small groups, not with their mothers and younger sisters. She'd be with Karen and Gemma now if she hadn't used up all her allowance when the month was only half gone. Or, to be more accurate, if Mum wasn't so stingey. The other girls always seemed to have money. It was Mum who ought to be a cheerful giver.

A girl of about sixteen walked past, wearing a supermarket overall. Must be her Saturday job, Claire decided. If only I was old enough to get a job, she thought. Or even, she told herself with growing resentment, if only Mum would let me stay in the house on my own while she went shopping with Alison.

Still, waiting out her time in the shopping centre was better than dragging round the supermarket. If she chose anything, Mum would say, 'I'm not buying those sugared cereals, they'll rot your teeth. You don't need that chocolate, it'll give you spots. Put those oven chips back, they're fattening.'

And Alison was the last straw – becoming vegetarian! Rotten little creep.

The cold of the wall was beginning to strike through the seat of her jeans, so Claire stood up and ambled disinterestedly to the far end of the shops. Not that the shops weren't interesting, just that it was completely pointless looking at them when you couldn't buy anything. Tantalising, too. There was a really nice fluffy, grey jumper in MacAllans', but Mum had pointed out, as usual, that both Claire and Alison had already had T-shirts and sweatshirts this month, and new trainers... And Mum was making her own posh outfit for Aunty Barbara's graduation ceremony, because she couldn't afford to buy one. Claire sighed.

At the very edge of the shopping area, where he wouldn't get moved on, was a busker. Claire quickened her pace. She liked buskers. They added a bit of colour to life in a shopping centre. Besides, they were *almost* illegal. But only almost. There was nothing wrong with busking. After all, no one was forced to pay a busker. You were free to give if you wanted to, and if you liked the music.

As she drew nearer, she could hear the musician more clearly. He was playing his guitar, and singing. His music wasn't really her type. The busker was definitely past it, and anyway, Claire suspected he'd never been very good. Just as well. She had three pence in her pocket, and she didn't have the cheek to give that. Huh, she thought. So much for cheerful giving.

She turned and moved slowly in the opposite direction. She had far too much time left. There was still half an hour to go before she was due to meet Mum and Alison.

At the opposite end of the shopping centre, she could hear more music – if that was the word for it. Once she could spot its source, she shuddered. An old man with one and a half legs was sitting on an angler's folding stool, playing a violin. At least, he was scraping the bow across the strings, which was not at all the same thing. The shoppers were giving him a wide berth, embarrassed by his dishevelled appearance, his deformity and the excruciating racket.

Taking refuge in a shop doorway, Claire stood and watched. As she listened, she began to recognise the tune he was playing. It was a march, one that the Scottish Fiddlers had learnt at school last year. It was 'The Lovat Scouts'. And he should follow it up with the Strathspey dance tune 'Miss Lyall', and finish with the reel 'Loch Leven Castle'. Claire held her breath. She loved those pieces. Having mastered them, and being able to play the reel up to its correct speed gave her a lot of satisfaction. She didn't want this old loser to mangle them. She looked at his hands. His finger joints were bumpy, like Granny's. No wonder he played so badly, Claire thought, crossly. He ought to give up. And sure enough, he did give up, before the reel. It gave the music an incomplete feeling, like chips without ketchup, or a birthday cake without candles.

Claire looked at her watch. Still twenty-five minutes to go. She was about to turn away when she saw the old man lay his fiddle down lovingly in its open case. It was a good instrument, she observed. The shoppers continued to pass him by, marching, dawdling, shuffling, hurrying. No one looked at him. With horror, Claire saw a furtive tear slide down his leathery cheek. It must be because he hadn't earned much money, she thought. But he wasn't looking at the cap with the few coppers in. He was looking at his fiddle. He leaned over and stroked it as it lay in its padded case. Then he spread his hands on his lap. They were bent and gnarled. He flexed his fingers, but they were clearly painful.

Suddenly, he looked up and caught Claire's eye. She looked away, embarrassed, but her gaze rested on the violin.

'Oh, yes, m'dear. It's a good one!' he said, reading her thoughts. His voice was more gentle and cultured than she had expected. 'I've had it fifty years,' he continued. 'Reckon I've taken better care of this instrument than I have of myself!' He gazed ruefully at his stump of a leg. Claire wanted to walk away, but somehow it would have seemed very rude. So she stood there, hoping no one who knew her would walk past.

'Do you play?' he asked suddenly. Claire nodded

reluctantly. 'Come and hold the instrument!' he invited, his face crinkling into a smile. Claire hung back. 'Come on! It's a beauty!'

At last, Claire stepped out of the refuge of the shop doorway and went across to the violin case, next to the old man. She glanced round self-consciously, to check no one was watching. Actually, she *did* want to handle the beautiful instrument. It drew her like a magnet.

One day, she thought longingly, one day, when I'm rich and famous, I'll be able to own an instrument like this.

With infinite care and respect, Claire lifted the fiddle from its case. She turned it over carefully, noticing the skilled way in which it had been made. She stroked her thumb across the strings, then picked up the bow. It was a fine, full bow, in good condition.

'How long have you been playing, m'dear?' the old man asked eagerly.

'Er, nearly seven years.'

'Classical, or Scottish fiddle?'

'Both. But I like Scottish fiddle best.'

'Have a go! Play something!'

'Oh, no!' Claire said, shocked. She began to lay the fiddle down again.

'I played at your age,' the old man went on quickly. 'Played in a Highland Strathspey and Reel Society. Set everyone's feet tapping, we did!'

Claire stood still, undecided.

'Try a few bars. Anything. So you can feel the quality of the instrument.'

She was hooked. She looked round once more and her heart skipped a beat. She'd spotted Shack

Robertson in the distance. She could hardly begin to imagine what *he* would say later, at school, if he saw her. But he was heading in the other direction, and concentrating on using his crutches. His ankle wasn't broken, just badly twisted after he had fallen in the cross-country race. But he seemed to think that crutches were cool. They certainly drew everyone's sympathy, especially the girls'.

Claire focused her attention on the violin. She tucked it under her chin and drew the bow across the strings in a full chord. The beautiful, mellow resonance filled her head. Then, oblivious to the passing shoppers, she launched into 'The Lovat Scouts'. As she played, she glanced at the old man. His face relaxed and a smile played around his mouth.

Facing him, her back to the walkway, Claire progressed into 'Miss Lyall', and as she came to the end of the piece, he looked at her with a mixture of curiosity and hope. Claire continued confidently into 'Loch Leven Castle' with all the trills, her fingers neat and accurate, her bow flying with expressive precision. Aware only of the music, the old man's alert face and his one tapping foot, Claire didn't even see the gathering crowd.

When eventually she finished with another full chord, a semi-circle of shoppers three deep had formed around her. Suddenly acutely embarrassed, she replaced the fiddle carefully in its case and stepped back, behind the old man, as if his bent form could shield her from the stares of amazement and admiration. As she did so, people began to come forward and put money in the old man's greasy cap.

Not just coppers, but silver – twenties, fifties and pounds. There was a blue fiver. Claire thought only fleetingly of the grey, fluffy jumper, then she slipped away into the crowd and made her way to the supermarket entrance, just as Mum and Alison emerged with a loaded trolley.

'Hello love!' Mum greeted her. 'Did we seem ages? Were you very bored? What did you do?'

'It was OK,' Claire replied truthfully. Then she added, 'I just moseyed around. There was this old guy playing Strathspey pieces on a fiddle.'

'Bet he wasn't as good as you!' Mum said.

'Oh, I expect he was once,' Claire mused. 'But he's a bit past it now. Did you get any Coke?' She began to poke into the shopping bags.

'We got fresh orange juice!' Alison retorted. 'It's healthier.'

They left the shopping centre and drove home, back past the old church building with its poster about a cheerful giver. Claire glanced at the poster, and smiled to herself.

The gig

'Four weeks! But that'll be after my birthday!' Karen fingered the cumbersome brace on her injured knee, and bit her lip to try to stop her chin trembling. 'And six more weeks with crutches!'

'All you need is a mask, and you'll look like Darth Vader!' her brother Jonathan commented unhelpfully.

'Good job we weren't planning to buy you a hockey stick, isn't it, love?' her mum joked, trying to lighten the atmosphere.

'You'll feel your knee getting better all the time, Karen,' Doctor Jenkins said sympathetically. 'Four weeks without putting your foot to the ground may seem like a long time now, and you won't be doing any disco dancing at your birthday party, but the operation you've had to repair your cartilage should ward off problems like arthritis when you're older.'

Karen nodded and blinked hard. 'Anyway,' the doctor added, 'if it's not a hockey stick, what *are* you hoping for, for your birthday?'

'A mobile phone,' Karen said bleakly.

'Well, you'll be able to phone us here on the ward after you get home, and tell us about your birthday!'

Karen nodded, and tried to smile. The doctor patted her hand and left. Karen's bravery dissolved, and she sobbed, 'But Mum, I won't be able to go to the Delirious? gig! Gemma will have to go without me!' She took her steamed-up glasses off and cleaned the lenses.

'I know, love,' Mum sympathised, 'but I'm sure there'll be another opportunity.'

'There won't, Mum. They'll never come to Edinburgh again!'

'Karen loves Jon Thatcher! Karen loves Jon Thatcher!' Jonathan chanted.

'Jonathan!' Mum warned.

'It's true!' Jonathan protested. 'She's got posters of him all over her bedroom walls!'

'*So*?' Karen challenged, tearfully.

'Well, maybe you could have a birthday party instead, or at least a few friends round,' Mum suggested soothingly.

'Gemma, any news of Karen?' Mr Nevis asked as soon as he'd closed the register book.

'Yes, I went to visit her in hospital yesterday evening,' Gemma replied. The whole class listened eagerly. Gemma stole a glance at Doug. He was all ears.

'Is her leg broken?' Jessica asked.

'No. She tore the cartilage in her knee, and part of it got trapped between two bones. That's why she couldn't straighten her leg.' A shudder went round the class.

'So did they remove the cartilage?' Mr Nevis inquired.

'No. They did an operation to repair it. They released it and sewed it up.'

'Is her leg in a big plaster, then?' Phil asked.

'No, not a plaster. She's got a big kind of brace thing. It lets her move her knee a bit, but she's not allowed to put any weight on it for a month. Then she'll have crutches for six weeks.'

'Ten weeks altogether! That's *worse* than a broken leg!' Doug breathed. Murmurs of agreement and sympathy rippled around the class.

'I'll buy a get well card and we can all sign it,' Mr Nevis announced. 'Do you know when she's coming out of hospital?'

'Tomorrow, I think,' Gemma replied. 'If we could do the card tomorrow, Holly and I could take it round after school.'

The bell went for first period, and everyone shuffled out of the classroom.

'Poor old Karen,' Holly said as they made their way along the crowded corridor. 'She won't be able to go to the Delirious? gig.'

'Oh!' Gemma imagined the concert venue, packed with enthusiastic, jostling people, all eager to secure a space at the front where they could jump up and down and cheer. Not a safe place for anyone on crutches. But the smallest flicker of an idea began in Gemma's imagination.

'Maybe you and Claire shouldn't go after all,' Holly suggested. 'Karen's the real Delirious? freak. You two were just going to keep her company, weren't you?'

'Well, yes,' Gemma admitted, 'but we've bought the tickets now, and anyway, Claire's really keen on all sorts of music. And I've never seen them live before.' Somehow, she didn't want to share her idea yet, not until she'd had time to think it out a bit more.

Karen was discharged from hospital the next day, and her mother made up a bed on the sofa, and supported her sore knee with pillows. Karen tried to smile and be grateful. All her get well cards were on the coffee table where she could see them and read them again. She picked up the one from the Resolution Club leaders, Bonnie and Tiny. Bonnie had got all the Resolution members to sign it. It was a smiling sun. Inside Bonnie had written, 'Hope we'll be seeing your sunny smile before too long.' Karen pulled a face. She didn't feel at all sunny. Bonnie had also written a Bible verse: 'We know that in all things God works for the good of those who love him'. Romans 8:28.

Then she'd added, 'God never stops loving us, even when we're injured. I pray that you'll know his love in a special way.'

How can God love me, Karen thought. Surely if he really loved me, he wouldn't have let this happen to me.

The day was long and boring, but at four o'clock, Gemma and Holly brought a card signed by the whole class. Karen opened it eagerly and searched for Doug's signature. He had written, 'Missing you. Get well soon. Love, Doug.'

Everything looked less bleak for a moment. 'Mum suggested I had a party instead of going to the gig...' Karen began tentatively. 'I was wondering if...'

'Couldn't you have it on a different day,' Gemma begged. 'Otherwise I won't be able to come...'

After Gemma and Holly had left, Karen whispered to herself over and over, 'In all things God works for the good of those who love him'. But it didn't seem to help.

'Gemma! How could you *do* that!' Holly exploded, as soon as they had left Karen's house. 'Karen's supposed to be one of your best friends, and you've chosen to go to a gig instead of to her birthday party!' When Holly was angry, her face became as red as her hair, and her freckles stood out. They were standing out now.

'But the gig was booked first. It's a prior engagement!'

'With two thousand people in the audience, Delirious? are not going to miss *you*!' Holly argued.

'But I've got an idea,' Gemma explained patiently. 'If I can set it up, Karen will like it much more than having me at her birthday party.'

'What idea?' Holly demanded.

'I'll tell you later, if it works. Anyway, you and Ella can go to the party, can't you?'

'Huh! It'd better be a jolly good idea!' Holly muttered crossly, and turned off down her own street towards home.

'What's up with her?' Jonathan demanded ten minutes later, coming in and flinging his school bag on to a chair.

'Karen?' Mum asked, concerned. 'What's the matter, love? I thought Gemma and Holly's visit might cheer you up?'

'Well, it did, sort of,' Karen sniffed. 'It's just that, well, I thought Gemma might come to my party, if I had one. But she says she's going to the gig anyway. But it's me that's the real Delirious? fan. She was only going to come to keep me company.'

In the days that followed, Karen's progress seemed very slow. She couldn't concentrate on the schoolwork which was sent home to prevent her from getting too left behind. She couldn't sleep properly because her knee was too sore. Friends' accounts of basketball matches, discos and cinema trips just made her feel worse.

She spent a lot of time in her room, staring at her Delirious? posters. Eventually, reaching up with one of her crutches, she pulled them off the wall, one by one, leaving only torn corners surrounding the drawing pins. She stopped when she got to the one of Jon Thatcher. She gazed into his gorgeous eyes. He beamed down at her with such warmth, and she tried to smile back, but her glasses steamed up and she had to look away.

'What are you wearing to Karen's party?' Gemma asked Holly as they packed their schoolbags before going home.

'Nothing special. It's not really a *party*. She's just having a few friends round for pizza and videos. She said not to wear anything posh because she can only wear baggy jeans that cover her knee brace.' Holly paused, then she added, 'Are you sure you won't change your mind, and come?'

'I've got a much better plan,' Gemma said mysteriously. Holly scowled. 'But it will only work properly if you play your part.'

Holly stared at her. She didn't look enthusiastic, but at least she stopped frowning. Gemma turned away to hide a smile, and continued organising her bag.

'What do I have to do, then?' Holly said finally.

Gemma grinned. 'You know how Karen said she's getting a new mobile phone for her birthday?'

'Yeah...'

'Well, what you have to do is find out her new number as soon as you arrive at her house, then phone me secretly and tell me it. Only don't tell her you're phoning me.'

'How am I going to do that if I've only just arrived?'

'Oh, make some excuse. Go to the loo, or pop into the kitchen and offer to help her mum. You'll think of something,' Gemma said confidently. 'And make sure she's got her phone switched on!'

When the big day arrived, Karen cheered up a bit. Friends, relatives and family sent lovely presents, cards and messages, and anyway, her knee was becoming a little more mobile. Ella, Holly and a few more friends were invited for pizza and videos, and Karen received more presents, and showed off her smart, new, silver mobile phone. She'd hoped that Gemma might have changed her mind at the last minute. After all, they'd been best friends since they were eight. But seven-thirty came and went, and as Karen's thoughts strayed to the Corn Exchange, where the gig was going to be, her friends laughed, joked and ate pizza. At ten minutes to eight, Karen imagined Gemma and Claire joining the chanting, swaying, cheering crowd inside. She thought about everyone jumping up and down. She pictured herself shouting, clapping, laughing and crying over her favourite band. She imagined Jon stepping on to the stage, picking up his guitar, his eyes locking into a gaze with hers...

Her dreams were disturbed by an unfamiliar electronic tune. 'Karen! Karen! Phone!' Her friends were shrieking at her. Confused, she looked around for the new phone. She dug under the cushion, and fumbled with the button.

'Er... hello?'

'Karen?' asked a male voice – strange, yet strangely familiar.

'Yes?'

'Jon Thatcher here! Gemma tells me you couldn't make it to the gig this evening. Well, God bless you, Karen. Keep that new silver phone switched on because this first song is for you!'

As Karen's friends crowded around the phone, Delirious?'s new single filled the air. Heads together, listening, Karen and her friends swayed in time to the music and cheered loudly as the song faded. 'Brilliant!' shouted Karen, punching the air.

In bed that evening, when her friends had gone and all the excitement had died down, Karen whispered to herself, thank you, Jon, thank you Gemma, thank you, Bonnie. And thank you, God.

Dithering

'Orange juice or apple juice?' Ella's mum demanded, standing beside the open fridge, a carton in each hand.

'Apple, please. No, orange. Oh, whatever!' Ella replied with a mouthful of toast. Her mum poured her a glass of orange juice, and sat down at the table.

'Look at these skirts,' she said, pushing a clothing catalogue across the table so Ella could see it. 'I thought of getting you one for our trip to Cairo. Which one do you like best?'

Ella looked at the pictures. She didn't really like any of them. 'They're too old for me, Mum. Skirts for old fogies!'

'Like me, you mean?'

'No!' But her mother was grinning. Ella relaxed. 'You know what I mean, Mum. Look at the models. They're all older women. Look at the skirts. Isn't there anything for younger people like *me*?'

'There are, but they're all either very mini, or they're meant to display your belly button. In Cairo, you have to dress very conservatively, or they don't think you're decent.' Ella pulled a face. 'You'd only have to wear the skirt for one holiday,' her mum coaxed.

'OK,' Ella agreed reluctantly. She chose a blue one. The fabrics looked really nice. It was just the style…

On the way to school she regretted her choice, and wished she'd opted for a yellow one. She tried to phone her mum, but couldn't get through.

At school, in PSHE, a visiting speaker told Mr Nevis's class about a community project which was asking for help from young people. He was cool and funny, and the class liked him instantly. 'You're all old enough to make a real contribution,' he told them. He showed them two short films. The first one was about handicapped children enjoying various sports with able-bodied teenagers, while the second one showed young people helping disabled people of all ages with crafts and painting. The films were excellent, and the speaker's enthusiasm was infectious. Everyone in the class was urged to opt for either sports or crafts. The project was to take one afternoon a week for eight weeks after the Easter holidays.

At lunchtime the dining hall was buzzing with excited chatter. Everyone Ella talked to wanted to do sports, but Ella had always preferred crafts.

'Choose sports, then we can be in the same group,' Gemma urged her.

'Hmm.' Ella turned to Karen. 'With your knee, you'll probably...'

'It'll be better by then!' Karen declared, bending and flexing her leg to prove it. 'Anyway, sport with these kids won't be about winning matches. It'll be more like making friends and helping them individually.'

'So will crafts!' Ella objected.

'Do sports! All the boys will choose the sports option!' Claire said confidently.

At the next table, Phil overheard, and turned to grin. It was true. Ella certainly knew which one Phil would choose. She chewed her lip. She enjoyed *watching* sport, especially when Phil was playing or if it was a Hearts v. Rangers match, but she had never been very good at games, and she could just imagine her embarrassment if the handicapped kids didn't want to play with *her* because she was no good. But she didn't want to be the *only* one choosing crafts. She couldn't make up her mind.

'When did you say you have to decide by?' Mum asked, standing in front of the mirror, holding up a light summer dress to her shoulders.

'After the holiday,' Ella replied.

'Oh, plenty of time, then. No need to panic yet.'

'But everyone else has made their decision already!' Ella complained.

'Well, what do you really want to do?'

'Crafts. You know I love art and design and stuff, and I'm no good at PE.'

'That's easy then. Go for crafts. What do you think of this dress?'

'Bit cold for March!'

'I mean for Cairo, silly. For our trip. It's always hot in Egypt.'

Ella sighed, exasperated. 'But Mum, if everyone else is doing sports, I might feel left out.'

'Who's everyone?'

'Oh, Claire and Karen, and Gemma… and Phil.'

'Oh. And Phil!' Mum smiled.

'It's not like that!' Ella said crossly. 'You know how good Phil is at sport.'

'Look, love, you just have to make a decision and stick to it.'

Put like that, it sounded easy. But how could you be sure you'd made the right decision? And if you thought you'd made the wrong one, *should* you stick to it? Ella knew she always dithered over small decisions. Whatever would she do when it came to big ones? Like GCSE subjects? Or a job? Or a husband? Ella shuddered.

Ella arrived at the Resolution Club at the same time as Phil and another boy. 'Hi, Ella. This is Jamie.' Ella smiled and said hello. 'Remember the Valentine's Day Cross-country Race?' Phil asked. Ella nodded. 'It was Jamie whose dog got hurt.'

'But he's fine, now,' Jamie smiled. 'His broken leg's as good as new.' Holly, Gemma and Doug arrived, and they all went in together. Bonnie was on the door, welcoming everyone, and getting them to sign in.

Ella looked around the hall. There were several inflated balloons on the platform. 'Somebody's birthday?' she asked Phil.

'Dunno,' he shrugged.

'OK everyone,' said Tiny, drawing himself up to his full six foot five, 'Hands up if you prefer ham and pineapple pizza to pepperoni!' Ella glanced around. About six hands went up. 'Right, who prefers pepperoni?' About the same number of hands went up.

'That'll do,' Tiny announced. 'Two teams – the ham and pineapples on this side and the pepperonis on that side!'

Everyone groaned. 'That's really mean, Tiny!' Holly complained.

'Why?' Tiny asked innocently, his grin giving him away.

'We thought we were getting pizza!' Ella told him.

The Resolution Club laughed good-naturedly. They all liked Tiny. He was cool.

'It's balloon volleyball, and this is the net.' He chalked a line across the floor. 'Bibles out, and turn to page 544. Psalm 15.' He told the two teams to read alternate verses aloud, shouting them to the opposite team, so everyone could hear. They faced each other, and read loud and clear.

'Lord, who may enter your Temple?
Who may worship on Zion, your sacred hill?
A person who obeys God in everything
and always does what is right,
whose words are true and sincere,
and who does not slander others.
He does no wrong to his friends
nor spreads rumours about his neighbours.'

'He despises those whom God rejects,
but honours those who obey the Lord.
He always does what he promises,
no matter how much it may cost.
He makes loans without charging interest
and cannot be bribed to testify against the innocent.
Whoever does these things will always be secure.'

'The pepperonis can start,' said Tiny, handing a balloon to Ella. 'Remember, bat the balloon around your own team members until you've worked out the answer to the question, and then hit it over the net as you shout the answer. One point for each right answer. Lose a point if everyone in the team hits it before you can answer.'

Each team spread out in their half of the hall, to give lots of thinking space.

'First question. What did the writer ask?'

Ella hit the balloon as high as she could, but Jamie was quick off the mark. 'Who can enter God's temple and worship on his special hill?'

'Yeah!' everyone cheered. Jamie hit the balloon to the opposite team.

'Question two,' said Tiny quickly. 'What sort of people can?'

'Can what?' Jamie asked, puzzled.

'Can worship on God's holy hill!' Holly explained for the ham and pineapples, hitting the balloon as high as she could. 'People who obey God.'

'Yes. And?' The balloon went across to the other side.

'People who tell the truth.'

'Yes. And?' Over went the balloon.

'People who don't spread gossip.'

'Well done. Some more?'

'People who respect other Christians.'

'Er, yes. That'll do. It says, "Those who obey the Lord". What else?'

'Don't take bribes.'

'Lend money.' The balloon was batted back and forth, back and forth with each right answer.

'Don't tell lies.'

'We've had that one. That doesn't count!'

'There's one more,' said Tiny. 'An important one

that you've missed.'

'Keep their promises whatever the cost!'

'Yes, that's it!' Tiny began. 'People who...'

'Ella!' the pepperonis yelled at her. 'What're you doing?'

'Sorry,' Ella said. She'd caught the balloon. 'I wasn't thinking. At least, I was. Er...'

'Round one to the ham and pineapples!' Tiny announced, taking the balloon from Ella and giving it to Jamie. 'You start this time, ham and pineapples. Round two, question one. What sort of promises do we have to keep?'

'Promises to our parents.'

'To be home on time.'

'To share things with your little sister. Ugh!'

'To do the washing up.'

'To walk the dog.'

'To tidy your room.'

'No!' Ella said crossly, catching the balloon on purpose. 'Those are stupid promises. Everyone has to tidy their room and do the washing up.'

'Ella, give us the balloon! You're spoiling the game!' Jamie said, attempting to snatch it from her.

'You're missing the *point* of the game!' she told him, trying to hang on to the balloon.

'Have you got a question, Ella?' Bonnie asked, stepping in before an argument developed.

'Well, yes. How can you be sure you've made the right promise? I mean, suppose you say you'll do something, then you think it was a mistake? Do you still have to keep your promise? And does God want you to make promises you don't even want to keep?'

'I take your point,' Tiny said thoughtfully. 'What does anyone else think?'

'I suppose it's always difficult to keep promises, otherwise there'd be no point in making them,' Holly suggested.

'Yeah, and it wouldn't say "No matter what the cost",' Phil agreed.

'What's more, God gives us gifts for a purpose,' Tiny added. 'He doesn't usually expect us to make promises to do the things we hate. Just to work hard at using our gifts to serve him.'

At least people are taking it seriously now, Ella thought, relieved.

'Maybe we should pray,' Tiny suggested, 'then finish the game off with some more questions, so we have a clear winner.' Ella closed her eyes. 'Lord God,' Tiny prayed, 'please help us to make the right decisions, and then to have the determination to stick by what we've promised, and not chicken out. Help us to recognise the gifts you've given us, and put them to good use even when the going gets tough. Amen.'

'Amen,' they chorused.

'And sometimes,' Tiny added after praying, 'if we ask him, God is extra kind to us, and reassures us we're making the right promises.'

I'll ask him, thought Ella, and felt happier than she'd felt all day.

The River Nile lived up to everyone's expectations. Ella could see it in the distance, a majestic silver ribbon, as they flew into Cairo airport. Their guest house was near the city centre. It wasn't quite the Hilton, but it was clean and comfortable.

On the first day, Ella's dad's business colleague met them in the entrance hall. 'Hello, Barry!' Dad said warmly. 'It's nice to see a familiar face in a foreign land! This is my wife, Lynn, and my daughter, Ella!'

'Pleased to meet you,' Barry said. 'You're in for a real treat today.'

He took them to see the Pyramids at Giza. They were more enormous than Ella could have imagined. 'However did they build them without modern technology?' Ella asked, amazed.

'Oh, you'd be surprised what people used to be able to do, even without technology!' her dad chuckled.

On one side of the Pyramids was nothing but desert, as far as the eye could see. On the other, the city had reached right up to them. 'Look, Mum,' Ella observed. 'Old and new, side by side!'

'Yes, love. And I expect the new learns from the old all the time. For a start, they should learn how to build things that last!'

In the middle of the tourist area the little group paused to look over the city stretching below them. Suddenly a wisp of song reached their ears and everyone held their breath to listen, entranced. The music increased as more and more voices joined in.

'It's the Muslim call to prayer!' Dad whispered, glancing at his watch. 'They pray regularly, five times a day.'

As the music reached a crescendo Ella thought it sounded mournful and haunting. She carried on walking, lost in thought.

In the cool of the early evening, when the Nile took on a rosy hue, Ella persuaded her parents to take a stroll. They walked south along the bank of the river. Although the traffic still roared close by, the street-sellers had packed up, and the city was as peaceful as it would ever get.

'Look!' Ella exclaimed. 'We could get through that gap in the shrubs and paddle! That'd be something, to paddle in the Nile!' She kicked off her sandals and scrambled through the gap. But as she straightened up, she was met by a scrawny old man wearing a dusty, torn shirt, and a piece of material wrapped round his waist like a skirt. He said nothing, and he was too old and bent to be a threat, but his dark eyes held a challenge. 'Oh, I'm sorry! I didn't realise... I mean, I...' She felt embarrassed and backed off. Just beyond the gap, pieces of cloth had been stretched across the bushes for a make-shift shelter. She could see the remains of a small fire, with a cooking pot beside it.

'I think we're intruding, love,' Dad said. 'Let's go back.'

Ella felt subdued. Back at the guest house, everything took on a different meaning. An ice-cold drink from the fridge was luxury. She realised she usually took everything for granted – clean water, food, shelter, safety. It made her feel uneasy.

During the remaining days, they sampled the local mint tea, ate couscous and delicious dried fruits, rode on the metro, and watched the old men who squatted on the pavement outside cafés, drinking coffee like sludge and smoking long, curly pipes.

While Dad and Barry had some business to do,

Ella and her mum went to Khalili Bazaar. They smelt the spices, listened to the stall-holders shouting their wares and admired the local crafts, leather work and mother-of-pearl jewellery boxes. Ella stood out of sight while another tourist bartered for his souvenirs. She checked her Egyptian money and did some sums. Five Egyptian pounds to one English one, so one Egyptian pound was worth about twenty pence. After the tourist had gone, she hissed, 'Hey, Mum! Watch this!'

She stepped into the middle of the stall, and held up a blouse to examine it carefully.

'Thees beautiful shirt, lady, eet very very nice for you!' The stall-holder smiled at Ella. His dark eyes twinkled, and his teeth flashed strong and white. He held it up against her shoulders. 'See! Very very nice! Eet cost feefty Egyptian pound. But for you, lady, only forty!'

'Forty Egyptian pounds?' said Ella. She pretended to be shocked, even though the man was only asking for eight pounds. 'I'd only pay twenty for it.' She started to turn away.

'Oh, lady! What you do to me! I 'ave wife and children to feed, you know?' He looked despairing. 'But for such a pretty face, maybe thirty-five?'

Ella turned back, pretending to be reluctant. 'Well, I don't know...' she muttered. Then she suggested, 'Thirty?'

'Thirty? Ees yours!' the stall-holder said, his face wreathed in smiles once more. Ella handed over the money and the pretty embroidered blouse was hers.

Ella and her mum moved off, giggling. 'That would cost twenty pounds at home, love,' Mum observed, 'and you've got it for about six quid!'

'I wonder how many children he *does* have to feed?' Ella mused.

'Now don't feel guilty about him,' Mum tried to reassure her. 'It's a game. He knew as well as you that you weren't going to pay forty.'

'All the same, some of the people are *very* poor,' Ella said sadly. She was still haunted by the reproachful dark eyes of the man on the river bank. She thought about heaven. It would surely have all the beauty of Cairo, but none of the poverty and injustice.

As they left the bazaar, a dozen small boys suddenly ran up to them, some reaching out grubby, empty hands, others trying to sell little trinkets – bracelets and necklaces.

'See, missy! For you! Very nice. Very cheap! You buy!' They pawed Ella's skirt and touched her arms. One of them tried to pull her hand. She shuddered and grabbed her mum's arm.

'Off you go!' Mum said firmly. 'We don't want to buy! No, thank you!'

Undaunted, the boys continued to chatter and run around them. They quickened their pace. Then a stern voice called in Arabic, and the boys disappeared instantly. Ella turned, and in a doorway leaned a handsome young man, smartly dressed and smiling at her.

'Good morning! Welcome to Egypt!' he called. Ella smiled uncertainly. He turned to her mother. 'Your beautiful daughter – a princess! How many camels?'

'Sorry, she's not for sale!' Mum laughed, and the

young man put on a tragic face. Then his smile returned, and he called, 'Have a good holiday!'

Chuckling, they went back to the guest house for some lunch.

Ella found the Cairo Museum fascinating. The statues were huge, the carvings intricate and the mummies a bit disgusting but not scary. Some of the relics from the tomb of Tutankhamen, the boy king, were on display in an air-conditioned room with a specially regulated temperature. Ella found them exquisitely lovely. There was jewellery and furniture, and utensils for the young king to use in the next life. It was much too late to tell Tutankhamen that he wouldn't be able to use them. What a contrast, Ella thought, between the rich boy king and the poor old man. But it wasn't too late, Ella was sure, to help the poor people who were still here. What can I do, Lord God, she thought with sudden longing, and how will I know?

On the last morning, Dad had bills to pay and Mum had packing to do. Barry offered to take Ella to see the refugee project. 'I thought you might be interested – craft and design and all that,' he beamed.

Ella followed him to the basement of the new cathedral where she found a hive of industry – a happy, colourful, noisy community surrounded by beautiful crafts. They were making baskets, table mats, floor rugs, hats and every type of souvenir, just like the ones she'd seen at Khalili Bazaar. They were using all sorts of different materials. The staff were international – Americans, British, Arabs, Sudanese. There seemed to be a mixture of languages, but communication obviously wasn't a problem.

'What we need,' one of the young American women told her, 'is young people with some skill, energy and imagination to come and work with us for a year. Projects like this really help the economy, and the quality of life for some of these folks. See that woman?' She indicated a tall young African weaving a rug. 'She comes from the Sudan. Her husband was killed. She was living on the rubbish dump, and her children were starving. Since she started working here she's found a room to rent, with running water. Her children have food and clothes. They come here sometimes. They're so cute.' They moved around so Ella could get a good look at everything. Barry joined them again.

'It's a great opportunity for the staff, as well as the workers,' he explained. 'A year in this sort of work really helps you understand what's what. Who knows...' he added mischievously, 'in a few years' time, when you've become an expert in art, craft and design, you might come and make a contribution here?' Ella smiled happily. It was a dream she'd love to hold on to.

When they emerged from the basement into the bright sunshine, everything was suddenly crystal clear for Ella. 'Thank you, Lord God,' she whispered. 'Thank you for showing me how I can use my gifts to help others. Please help me to stick to my decision.'

Friends

Claire brushed her hair and leaned close to the mirror to apply concealer to an annoying spot on her forehead. Then she stood back and looked at herself critically. Not bad, she had to admit. Brushing her hair never had made much difference, but a school photographer had once said she had fine bone structure, so she tilted her chin in order to see her profile. Back to full face, she pouted and tried to look appealing, and finally she grinned broadly, the way you do for holiday snaps.

She glanced round guiltily, in case anyone was looking, but her bedroom door was shut, she had heard Alison go downstairs and Mum was clattering in the kitchen.

Claire rearranged the things on top of her dressing table, then looked at the Bible verses she had stuck around her mirror. She liked to copy out her favourite verses on Post-it notes and stick them up in her room. Her current favourite passage was Psalm 139. She had written out several verses: 'O Lord, you have searched me and you know me' and 'I praise you because I am fearfully and wonderfully made' and 'How precious to me are your thoughts, O God'.

Tiny had read the whole psalm to them at the Resolution Club one Friday evening, and told them that God was thinking about them all the time. He was always with them, and he knew everyone's situation perfectly. He understood when they felt happy or sad, proud or ashamed, hopeful or discouraged. Nothing, good or bad, could ever surprise him.

'Come on, Claire! Breakfast!' Mum called.

Grabbing her sports bag, Claire pushed her swimsuit and towel into it, then her hairbrush and deodorant. She picked up her school bag with her books in, and ran downstairs.

There was some excitement as Mr Harrington, the swimming teacher, and the class gathered outside the school gates waiting for the bus. The Town Tub, as they called it, had closed down in favour of the new local leisure centre, and their weekly swimming lesson had been relocated. The pool was beautiful, the show-ers and changing rooms luxurious and there was lots of mirror space with coin-in-the-slot hair dryers. Since it was a shorter bus ride, they had five minutes extra after the lesson to buy chocolate bars from the machine, or a cappuccino from the sparkling new café.

Claire nibbled her chocolate and looked round the facilities. A couple of the pool attendants crossed the foyer, talking and laughing together. One of them was tall and good-looking, with a dazzling smile. 'Who's that?' Claire whispered to Ella, pointing with her chin and trying not to be too obvious.

Ella took the hint and looked sideways. 'That's Daleep, Arun's brother,' she told Claire. 'Gorgeous, isn't he?'

Claire forgot to be subtle, and stared, first at Daleep as he turned away down the corridor, then at Arun. Apart from their colouring and big dark eyes, there was no comparison. Arun was skinny and quite small. There were some twelve-year-olds bigger than him. But Daleep looked strong and his smile had been warm and confident. Claire wondered if Arun would ever look like his brother. Arun must have been aware of her staring, because he turned to look at her. She looked away, embarrassed.

'How old is he?' she whispered to Ella.

'Eighteen, I think. Too old for you!' Ella joked.

'No, I wasn't... I mean, I didn't...' But Mr Harrington was moving everyone out and Ella wasn't listening.

The following week, Daleep was sitting in the high life-guard's chair while Claire's class had their lesson. Claire knew he would have a very clear view of every swimmer from up there. She watched the others swimming up and down. Shack made a tremendous splash but he was fast. Ella wasn't fast, but she swam like a ballet dancer. Holly preferred to swim with one foot on the bottom of the pool, and didn't mind when everyone laughed at her. But Jessica! Jessica swam like a fish, overtaking Greg with hardly a ripple, the water slithering easily over her skin.

Self-consciously, Claire swam down the length. She was aware of her limbs thrashing untidily, her mouth wide, gasping unnecessarily. She had never been particularly interested in swimming. It was good fun in the holidays, especially in the sea, when everyone splashed and shouted, jumping the waves. But when it came to serious sport, Claire's game was badminton. There, she shone. She was graceful, fast and strong.

Wishing she was on a badminton court now, Claire

tried too hard to swim elegantly. Her arms became tense, she ran out of breath, and finally grabbed the rail at the side, puffing and blowing.

'OK, Claire?' Mr Harrington asked anxiously, bending down to the pool-side.

'Yes thanks. Just a bit out of breath.' Claire didn't dare look up. She felt sure Daleep must be looking at her. She felt stupid, just when she wanted to look good. She was glad when the lesson came to an end.

While everyone was eating their snack before catching the bus back to school, Claire wandered around the foyer. She picked up a leaflet which gave a list of all the activities on offer at the centre. She looked at it on the bus on the way back to school. 'Under-sixteens badminton: Thursdays 7–9 pm', she read. 'New players welcome.'

'What're you dreaming about?' Ella asked. 'You were miles away!'

Claire smiled. She felt guilty, somehow. She'd been dreaming about getting badminton coaching from Daleep.

'Fancy joining the badminton club?' Ella continued, peering at the leaflet Claire was reading.

'Yes, only it's on a Thursday. That's orchestra night.'

'Well, you can hire a badminton court with friends on any other evening,' Ella pointed out. 'I'd quite like a game sometimes.'

'Mum!' Claire called, bursting in at the back door and dumping her school bag on the kitchen floor. 'The new leisure centre is great, and you can even hire a badminton court. You just pay for an hour at a time.'

'Let's see,' her mum smiled, looking up from the sewing machine which she had set up at the kitchen table, and taking the leaflet from Claire. 'Pretty pricey though, love. I think you'll have to be content with the occasional lesson at school.' She turned her attention back to the sewing machine. 'I can't seem to get these pleats right,' she sighed.

'Why don't you *buy* a dress for Aunty Barbara's graduation, Mum? You've never *enjoyed* sewing.'

'Do you know how much they cost?' her mum said, annoyed. 'I could never afford those sorts of prices. Anyway, if I make my own, I can get it to fit me exactly...' She didn't sound convinced.

'Why don't you get a full-time job, Mum? Then we'd have more money...' They'd had this conversation before, but Claire thought it was worth trying again.

'And give you and Alison a door key, so you could let yourselves in and cook your own tea, and do the cleaning and ironing...'

'OK, OK,' Claire muttered, going upstairs to her room. She sat on the edge of her bed and stared into her mirror. Then she read her verses from Psalm 139 again: 'How precious to me are your thoughts, O God'. She wondered if God's plans for her included a boyfriend. She imagined going for a pizza with Daleep; she pictured him waiting for her after school; she saw herself walking hand in hand with him...

She thought about Ella. She knew Ella and Phil had been out to the cinema together, and they always did things together at school. And she knew that Arun fancied Jessica. Ella had told her. In fact, they'd giggled about it privately, because Jessica was about twice as big as Arun. But the boys in her class seemed so young. Age difference wasn't important. She knew, for example, that Uncle Hal was six years older than Aunty Barbara.

Picking up a magazine, Claire looked at the photos of pop stars and film personalities, all smiling confidently. They were never short of boyfriends or girlfriends. One photo showed a black guy and a blond girl together. Their contrasting hair and skin looked fantastic. Claire stood up and lounged against the dressing table, trying to stick her bust out, imagining Daleep's arm around her shoulder, hers around his waist…

On Monday evening, Claire persuaded Ella to go swimming. Afterwards, they sat in the café overlooking the pool, drinking hot chocolate. Claire made hers last as long as she could, even though Ella was ready to leave. Her patience was rewarded when Daleep came in, obviously looking around for someone. He must have recognised them, because he smiled as he walked past, and said 'Hi, girls. All right?'

Claire nodded and smiled back. But he was gone immediately, and reluctantly, she drained her cup and picked up her bag. She and Ella stood up to leave, but on the way out past the counter, Claire picked up a leaflet with the pool opening times on it. She had an idea.

When she made an arrangement with Ella the following Monday, Claire suggested they went a bit later. 'I ought to do my homework and violin practice first,' she explained.

'But the pool closes at eight-thirty,' Ella pointed out, 'and you have to be out of the centre by nine.'

'We can go in at seven-thirty,' Claire said. 'It's a bit less crowded then, anyway. All the little kids leave earlier. That'll still give us chance for a good swim, and a shower and a drink in the café afterwards.'

They sat in the café and drank hot chocolate until one of the staff came round and said good-naturedly, 'Chuck-out time, girls, unless you want to help us wash the floors and clean the toilets! We're on till ten o'clock.'

'No, it's OK, thanks,' Ella said, grinning.

Claire was disappointed. She hadn't realised the staff stayed later. She thought they might catch the same bus home as Daleep.

Her big break came the following week at school. Miss Hall, the biology teacher, had made an arrangement with Mr Harrington. 'You can begin this work at your next swimming lesson,' she explained. 'Mr Harrington has agreed to give you some time specially for it. You'll need to measure each other's pulse and breathing *before* exercise, then again *afterwards*. The exercise has to be graded: gentle, medium and hard. It's best to choose a partner of similar ability when it comes to swimming.' She explained more tests at length, and concluded, 'Remember to write up your results in graph form as well as in writing. You might have to arrange for a time to meet outside school. All the instructions are on these sheets.'

At the swimming pool, Mr Harrington checked that they all had partners. Ella teamed up with Phil, while Karen, sitting on the pool-side with her knee brace, made a three with Gemma and Doug. Claire looked around. Arun was standing shivering, even though the atmosphere was quite warm. His ribs stood out, and his knees quivered up and down. Claire followed his gaze. He was looking at Jessica, but Mr Harrington was busy pairing Jessica off with Shack.

Suddenly, Claire saw her opportunity. Arun was only average at swimming, like herself. And if they had to finish the work off for homework, maybe they could do it at Arun's house, and maybe Daleep would be there...

Arun was good to work with. He was quick but careful, and Claire was impressed by the precision of his test results. 'Are you free to come round after school so we can write it up?' he asked her as they waited for the bus back to school. She phoned her mum to explain.

It was strange getting the bus home with Arun. Claire wondered what their home would be like and whether they usually spoke a different language. She didn't really know Arun at all.

Arun paused at the entrance to a block of flats, then seemed to take a deep breath and square his shoulders. 'In here,' he said, and led Claire through the lobby to the stairway. Two boys and a girl stood beside the bins, smoking and laughing together. They stopped and stared as Arun and Claire walked briskly past, but they didn't say anything. When they were out of sight but not out of earshot, they started to whistle and giggle.

'Who are they?' Claire asked.

'Oh, no one special,' Arun said airily. 'They're the local gang. They call themselves The Nails. They think they're really hard.'

Arun took out his front door key and opened the door to the flat. The entrance hall was tiny, and the door to the sitting room was open. 'Mum, this is Claire,' Arun said. He turned to Claire. 'This is my mum, and my sister, Nandita.' A girl older than Arun, but with the same wonderful even teeth as Daleep turned and flashed a smile at Claire. She was wearing a beautiful jacket of a heavy brocade material, and Arun's mother, in a colourful sari, was on her knees, making some alterations to the jacket. She stood up as Claire came in.

'Hello, dear. Very pleased to meet you,' she said. Nandita took the jacket off and went towards the kitchen. 'Like a Coke, Claire?' she asked.

'Yes, please.' Claire looked round the room. It looked pretty ordinary, except for a couple of pictures of wonderful exotic beaches with blue sea and palm trees. There was a very pretty crocheted lace cloth on the coffee table. The room smelt of furniture polish.

Arun's mum was busy clearing sewing things off the sofa so Claire could sit down.

'No, Mum, we need to sit at the table,' Arun corrected her. 'We need to draw a graph and write up some experiments.'

'Sorry,' she said quietly, seeming embarrassed. 'Not much space…'

Claire felt she ought to say something. 'Do you like sewing, Mrs Banerji? My mum does, too. At least, she doesn't particularly enjoy it, but she does it anyway…'

'Mum loves it! She's an expert!' Arun said proudly.

Claire had been going to add that her mum couldn't afford to buy posh clothes from the shops, but she thought she might be betraying family secrets. But she suddenly felt at home in this family. They probably didn't have much money, either, but they were trying to make her feel welcome.

Arun followed Nandita into the kitchen for a moment, and came out with a packet of chocolate biscuits. Nandita put two Cokes down on the table and Claire and Arun spread their books and papers out and got down to work.

'Mum, we need some stiffening for the collar,' Nandita told her mother, fingering the jacket thoughtfully.

'If you go to the shop in...' her mother began.

'Come with me, Mum, I'm sure to get the wrong stuff otherwise,' Nandita begged.

Finally, her mother agreed, and they went out, closing the flat door behind them. 'Mum doesn't get out enough,' Arun explained. 'She always complains that she doesn't know anyone, or doesn't have any friends, but she won't go out. Occasionally, Nandita manages to persuade her. But only if she goes *with* her.'

Claire and Arun discussed and planned for a while, then got on with writing up their notes. Arun was meticulous, drawing an accurate graph with a very sharp pencil, not chatting or interrupting their concentration.

The phone rang, disturbing Claire's thoughts, and just as she expected Arun to get up and answer it, a bedroom door opened and Daleep appeared and picked it up. Claire jumped. She had thought no one else was in. Her vague hope had come true. There she was, in Arun's flat, doing homework in the hope of meeting Daleep there. Her heart began to hammer. What now?

It was impossible, in a small flat, not to listen in to someone's phone conversation. When he had finished, Daleep put the phone down and groaned. Then he turned, nodded to Claire and said to Arun, 'That was Jack. He's got to meet his sister from Glasgow airport. Wants me to go in and finish the shift for him.'

'But you're meant to be off today!' Arun said.

'He did one for me last week. I can't get out of it, really. Anyway, he's only on till nine o'clock tonight. But I'm starving. I was planning to eat before going out later. Is there anything I can eat now, before I go?' He wandered into the kitchen. Arun followed him. 'I got these chicken pies out of the freezer,' he said.

'Why two?'

'I was going to cook them for Claire and me, if she wanted.'

Claire couldn't help overhearing. She went into the kitchen. She was quite touched that Arun had thought to offer her a chicken pie, but she was even more eager to give hers to Daleep. It would be the first thing she'd ever been able to give him. 'Sorry, couldn't help overhearing! You have it,' she said to Daleep. 'My mum will be cooking later on, and she'll be miffed if I'm not hungry enough to eat it.'

'OK, thanks,' Daleep said, putting the pies into

the microwave oven. 'Want yours now, Arun?'

'Yep. I'm always hungry enough to eat whatever Mum cooks,' he joked.

The two of them ate their pies, while Claire finished off her part of the graph. Arun admired Claire's handiwork, then said to Daleep, 'If you're going down now...'

'Yes. Claire can come down with me if she likes.'

Claire's heart missed a beat. 'It's The Nails,' Arun said vaguely. 'They can be stupid. You'll be OK if you go down with Daleep.'

'Right,' Claire said, packing her things away quickly, not wanting to miss whatever opportunity was coming her way.

Daleep grabbed his jacket and opened the door for her. They walked briskly down the stairs together and the boys and girl in the lobby actually stepped aside for them, but not without staring at Daleep, and looking Claire up and down slowly as she walked to the outer door. 'Take no notice of them,' Daleep said easily. 'They like to think they're hard, but they're soft as putty, really.' He made a fist with one hand and punched the other hand with it, grinning at Claire as he did so. She grinned back. She wouldn't be scared of anyone or anything if she was with Daleep.

Daleep caught a bus to the leisure centre, but not before walking Claire to her stop, and leaving her with her heart singing. In her bedroom at home, she stood in front of the mirror and practised her warmest smile. Thank you, Lord, she prayed. Thank you for thinking of me.

Mum cooked spaghetti bolognese, and while they

were eating it, Claire chatted about the biology experiment, and about writing it up at Arun's house. She talked about the beautiful jacket that Arun's mum was making, and about how neatly and precisely Arun did his work.

'Why are you so happy,' Alison asked, 'if all you've been doing is homework?'

Claire felt her cheeks grow hot, and said lamely, 'It was a really interesting project.'

After the meal, she went up to her room and emptied her school bag. As she was sorting her books and papers, she found to her horror that she had packed one of the papers Arun would need to finish his part of the project. It was due to be handed in the next day, and Claire knew Arun wouldn't want to be told off for handing in work late, especially if it wasn't his fault. She thought about getting a bus to Arun's house, but it was quite a long way. And The Nails might be there.

Then she had a brainwave! She'd get a bus to the leisure centre and give the paper to Daleep. That way, Arun would have time to finish it and she'd show Daleep how thoughtful and conscientious she could be.

She told her mum what she was going to do, but before she left, she spent a while in front of the mirror, putting on mascara and lipstick. Then she called goodbye from the hall and shut the front door behind her before Alison could comment.

It was dark, but the leisure centre was well lit. Claire couldn't decide whether to go in through the big main door, or to use the small side door which the staff used, hoping she might just catch Daleep on his own, without having to ask at the desk.

The side door had three steps, and a railing leading up to it. As she stood still, considering, it opened, and someone burst out of it, doubled over, clutching his stomach with one hand and the railing with the other. Claire stepped back into the shadow. Perhaps the figure was drunk. Whoever it was groaned, gasped, and, leaning over the railing, threw up. Vomit splashed on to the paving slabs. Horrified and disgusted, Claire prepared to run. The figure threw up again, then turned to sink on to the step, sitting with his head between his knees. In that moment, light from the lamp-post shone on to his face. It was Daleep. He moaned and pushed back his hair. Sweat glistened on his forehead, and in the lamplight his face was ghostly pale.

Claire gasped, and Daleep was suddenly aware that someone was there. He peered into the shadow. Now she could see his face clearly. He didn't look strong and invincible any more. He looked no older than Arun, despite his size, and suddenly Claire remembered how Mum always sat by her bed when she was ill, holding her hand and wiping her face with a cold, wet cloth.

Claire started forward. 'Claire?' Daleep asked hoarsely.

'Yes.'

'Sorry…'

'It's OK.' She was sitting on the step beside him now, bracing him with her shoulder, while he held on to the railing with his other hand.

'Need tissues,' he muttered, and she got up quickly and went inside, appearing a moment later with pieces of toilet roll and a couple of paper towels. She had wet one of them with cold water, and she laid it gently on his forehead and smoothed his hair back.

After a minute or two, he was sick again, standing up, turning away from her, trying to be as discreet as he could. Claire shut her eyes and put her hand over her mouth and nose. When he sat down again, he said, 'Feel a bit better now. Sorry about that. Ugh.'

Claire fished a bottle of water out of her bag and handed it to him. When he had taken a swig, she said, 'Keep it. I don't want it back!' and in spite of everything, they laughed for a moment.

'I'll go in and tell them you should go home,' she offered after a minute or two, and Daleep nodded.

Inside the leisure centre, Claire found the person in charge and told him what had happened. He came outside and patted Daleep on the shoulder. 'Don't come back till you're really better, lad,' he said kindly. 'Better take his things,' he said to Claire, handing her Daleep's sports bag and jacket.

They walked very slowly to the bus stop, and Claire kept close to Daleep in case he needed to lean on someone. When the bus came, she got on with him and bought tickets for both of them. 'Better sit next to the door, just in case,' she said. But Daleep wasn't sick again. He made no attempt to take his things from Claire when they got off the bus and she walked to his flat with him and up the stairs. There was no sign of The Nails. They must have found something better to do.

At the flat, Daleep let himself in and Claire hovered outside the door. Mrs Banerji took one look at him and pulled him inside. 'Not another!' she said, fussing around him. 'Arun's been throwing up all evening! It was the chicken pies! You didn't thaw them properly, and then you didn't cook them thoroughly.' She spotted Claire. 'And you, dear girl! Did you have a chicken pie, too?'

'No,' Claire replied, realising what a lucky escape she'd had.

'Come in a minute, dear. It's not catching!' Mrs Banerji assured her. Claire shuffled in and perched on the edge of an armchair. Daleep flopped on to the sofa beside Arun.

'Hi,' Claire said awkwardly to Arun. 'Sorry you're not well.' Arun turned glazed eyes towards her and attempted a smile.

'It was my fault,' he muttered. 'Food and Consumer Technology was never my strong subject!'

Claire grinned, remembering the burst flour bag. 'I haven't seen you look so pale since the day of…'

'Yeah, I know,' he interrupted, glancing towards his mum. Claire took the hint and didn't say any more.

The flat door opened again, and Mr Banerji arrived home. Claire had never met him before, so there were introductions all around.

There wasn't much room in the small flat, so Claire put Daleep's bag and jacket down and stood up to go. 'You've been a real friend, dear girl,' Mrs Banerji said. 'I wish we could do something to help you or your family…'

Claire smiled and thanked her, then had a sudden idea. 'Well, you might be able to.' Mrs Banerji looked up, interested. Arun and Daleep looked as well. 'My mum's trying to make this posh dress for my aunty's graduation ceremony, and it doesn't seem to be going very well. I think she needs some help from someone who knows about sewing.'

'Please bring her round. I'd be delighted to try and help!' Mrs Banerji said. And Claire could tell that she meant it.

Back home, Claire sat in front of her mirror and took her make-up off with face cleanser and cotton wool. She stared long and hard at her reflection. She wondered if you could still fancy anyone after watching them throw up. She guessed it must be possible, but not for her. At least, not yet. It had been a long day, but she felt surprisingly good. A one-way relationship was a lot of hassle. Instead, she felt she had gained a friend. Several, in fact. A whole family of friends.

She picked up her Bible and turned to her favourite psalm. Reading the last part, she turned it into her own prayer: 'Search me, O God, and know my heart; test me and know my anxious thoughts. See if there is any offensive way in me, and lead me in the way everlasting.' And Lord,' she added, 'I hope there'll be a boyfriend somewhere along the way, but I'm not in any rush.'

Before going to bed, she emptied her school bag, ready to pack it for the next day, and found the paper Arun would need to complete the biology project.

Dolphins

Jessica stood in the wings, shaking with nerves, waiting for her cue. June the first. Day of the dress rehearsal. She'd been dreading it for weeks. Might as well be April the first. She desperately didn't want to make a fool of herself. She took some deep, slow breaths, and went over her words: 'Romeo! Romeo! Wherefore art thou Romeo? Deny thy father and refuse thy name...'

Hidden behind a curtain, she could overhear Sasha and Angie gossiping. She knew they were just jealous, but that didn't make it any easier.

'You should've seen Shack Robertson's face when he heard he was going to be Romeo, and *she* was going to be Juliet!' Sasha whispered. Jessica could hear them sniggering.

'She only got the part because Miss Brown recommended her to Mr Nevis,' Angie hissed.

'What, Miss Brown the dance teacher?'

'Yep. Jessica used to be in the dance troop, you know. Miss Brown said she was a good mover.'

'Like Dumbo, you mean?' Sasha snorted.

Jessica knew why she'd been picked. She had a good, loud voice, and she wasn't scared. At least, that's what everyone thought. She'd spent years building up her street cred, making everyone believe she wasn't frightened of anything at all. It was true that she wasn't scared of any of the kids in the playground. She could make mincemeat of most of them, and she'd proved it once or twice, until she'd begun to understand more about anger, and how Jesus could help her with it. But a whole audience was a different matter. *They* could make mincemeat of *her*. And they probably would.

It was true, she used to dance. She'd grown too heavy for ballet in primary school, but she'd transferred to disco and jazz and been a star for a while. Miss Brown reckoned it was her natural Caribbean sense of rhythm. Then she became too aware of her body and felt too shy to dance any more. Right now, she felt miserable and very lonely.

'Ready, Jess?' Mr Nevis asked. 'Don't worry. It's only the dress rehearsal.'

Exactly, Jessica thought. If it had been the real thing, for mums and dads, it would have been OK. They always liked things. But the whole of her year was out there. Nearly two hundred kids. They would probably eat her alive.

'Remember, Jess. Up on to the balcony. One step forward. Pause, and speak! Up you go now!'

Jessica climbed cautiously up the stepladder that led to the scene's balcony, holding her long dress out of the way of her feet. She always felt awkward in anything but joggers and a T-shirt, and here she was wearing some flimsy, floaty thing, slung over one shoulder and held on with tacking stitches and pins.

She reached the top step, and ventured out along the plank.

Step. Pause. Speak! 'Romeo! Romeo! Wherefore art thou Romeo?' Her voice wobbled. Someone in the audience giggled. The hem of the dress was caught. Jessica shuffled, trying to free it. There was an ear-piercing crack, and she made a grab for the curtain just as the entire balcony collapsed. She fell, tangled up in the dress and the curtain.

There was a horrified silence, and everyone held their breath. Then Jessica fought her way from under curtains and pieces of wood with one knee scraped and her pride in tatters. Her floaty dress had been torn off in the fall, and she found herself alone in the middle of the stage in her bra and pants.

There was another split second's silence, then the whole room erupted in shrieks of delight. Jessica fled to the costume room, pulled on her joggers and T-shirt, grabbed her school bag in one hand and her trainers in the other, and ran for her life, unaware of Mr Nevis's concerned voice behind her. 'Jess! Any damage done? Jessica!'

Jessica sprinted out of the building, pausing at the school gates only long enough to stuff her feet into her trainers, Then she ran home and arrived shocked and breathless.

'Hello, honey!' said her mum, looking up from a casserole of something hot and spicy. 'Been running? You're early! How did the dress rehearsal go?'

'Er, the scenery wasn't ready, so we didn't do it all.'

'I'm so looking forward to tomorrow,' Mum said happily. She loved performances. She dressed up for every occasion, and made an entrance like the Queen of Sheba, just as if it were *she* who was on the stage. Just thinking about it made Jessica cringe. 'I know I've seen you in lots of dance shows,' Mum went on, 'but this will be your first *play*!' The phone rang, and Mum went into the hall to answer it. Jessica fled to her bedroom. How was she ever going to tell Mum that she wouldn't be acting tomorrow evening, or ever again? In fact, she was never, ever going to set foot in that school again in her whole life!

'Jessica?' Mum was lumbering up the stairs. 'That was the school. They said you'd fallen. They wanted to know if you're OK.'

Jessica wanted to cry, but since she never cried she kicked the foot of her bed so hard it made the wall shake. Mum demanded to know what was wrong. Since Jessica's mum was heavier than Jessica and as immovable as a brick wall, Jessica had no choice but to describe the whole afternoon to her, all except for the dress. 'I think the scenery collapsed because I'm too fat and heavy for it. It was designed for Juliet, not for an elephant!' she growled.

'Now let's get one thing straight!' said Mum firmly. 'You're not fat! You're strong and fit and healthy. All the swimmin' and joggin' you do has made muscle, not fat. And you're a very graceful mover. Miss Brown always said so. And just because you're not the right build for ballet any more doesn't mean you aren't very gifted!'

'Maybe I'll become a gifted demolition expert,' Jessica sniffed.

'Silly!' Mum said, giving her a hug. 'Something'll turn up. Every cloud has a silver linin'. Now come down and have somethin' to eat.'

'I'll be down in a minute, Mum. I'll just get changed.' But when Mum had gone, the full horror of the gossip and the laughter hit Jessica again. Mum didn't have to listen to Sasha and Angie being rude, or face Shack Robertson, or cope with the whole year talking about her knickers. And they surely would. Endlessly. She sat miserably on her bed and looked around. She'd forgotten to turn the page of her calendar. It was still on May. She looked at the picture. It was a mother hen gathering her chicks safely under her wing while outside the wire of the hen-house was a fox who couldn't get at them. There was a Bible verse underneath: 'Hide me in the shadow of your wings.' The calendar was from Aunty Ali. She always sent calendars and cards with Bible verses on them.

Jessica flipped the page to June, and the picture was a cartoon. There was a guy who was obviously full of himself, standing tall and arrogant, and a little, shy, dumpy figure, afraid to look up. But the sun was shining brightly on the second figure, and the Bible verse read, 'People judge others by what they look like, but the Lord judges people by what is in their hearts.' That's all very well, Lord, Jessica thought. But what's the good of wantin' to do things well, and havin' a beautiful heart, if you just look like a puddin'?

Having changed and washed her face Jessica went downstairs, but the smell of spicy chicken and pineapple didn't do anything for her. 'I don't think I need any food just now, Mum.'

'What's the matter, love? You sickenin' for something?'

Sickening. Yes, that was the word. Jessica rushed out of the room and threw up in the loo.

The next day was Thursday, and Jessica didn't actually feel sick at all, but she figured that if she remained ill she didn't have to go to school, and her understudy could play Juliet. It gave her time to think out some sort of strategy. So she said she felt queasy and refused breakfast and lunch. Her sister, Marina, looked disbelieving, but didn't grass on her.

Jessica stuffed yesterday's pants and bra into her waste bin, hoping never to set eyes on them again, but beyond that she had no idea what to do. She could run away, but that wouldn't be fair on Mum, and anyway, where would she go?

Maybe she could change schools? But the next nearest one was two bus rides away, in a rough area. Back to square one in building up the street cred. Jessica shuddered.

On Friday and Saturday she stayed in her room, though she did go down to the kitchen for meals. 'Why don't you go out for a gentle jog?' Mum suggested. 'A bit of fresh air might do you good.'

Jessica scowled. 'I might meet someone who... who...'

On Sunday afternoon, Mum said brightly, 'Remember Sylvia from work?' Jessica nodded. 'She's a member of the Country Club Leisure Complex. She can get guests in for just a couple of pounds to use the pool. Do you want to go?'

Jessica wavered. She'd love a swim, and she'd be unlikely to meet anyone she knew at the Country Club. It was mostly posh people who went there. 'There's a sauna, and a jacuzzi,' Mum added. Mum was planning to swim, and the sight of Jessica's mother in a swimsuit was enough to draw attention away from Jessica.

'OK. I'll get my things.' She wondered if Mum would tell Sylvia about *Romeo and Juliet*.

The Country Club pool was beautiful. There were flumes and a kids' pool, a diving area, and plenty of room for real swimming. Palm trees and tables around the edge made it more like the Caribbean than Scotland. It reminded Jessica of photos of Jamaica. Home, Mum always called it.

Mum and Sylvia chatted at the shallow end while Jessica dived into the deep end and raced up and down the length, revelling in fast action after so many days of inactivity. The pool was almost empty. Jessica dived again and again, swimming almost a length underwater before coming up for air, then turning and varying her strokes – crawl, butterfly, breaststroke, life-saving backstroke. She imagined pearl divers aiming as deep as they could, over and over, in the hope of a perfect pearl. She'd heard that some could last four minutes without a breath. She thought of turquoise sea, soft white sand and pink coral. She dived and glided, then twisted and somersaulted in a personal underwater acrobatic display.

When she came up for air, Mum and Sylvia were heading for the sauna. A girl about Jessica's age seemed to be watching her from the edge of the pool. Jessica shook the water out of her eyes and peered. With relief, she felt certain she didn't know her, so she dived again, enjoying being alone.

Next time she paused there was a young woman with the girl, and they were definitely looking at her. In panic, Jessica wondered if she was doing something wrong. She was wearing a wrist-band, she'd showered before swimming, there wasn't a NO DIVING sign. What could it be? But the young woman smiled, and the girl slid gracefully into the water and swam up to Jessica.

'Hi!' she said, 'I'm Anna. Sorry to stare at you like that. It's just that you, well, the way you were diving... I mean, you're brilliant!' She laughed. 'No, really! Where did you learn to swim like that?'

'I, er, well, I learnt to swim when I was little,' Jessica stuttered, 'but I don't know...' They arrived at the side of the pool. The young woman who was with Anna squatted down. 'Hello, I'm Carrie. I coach the synchronised swimming team, and Anna came to fetch me because she said you're a natural! And from what I've just seen, she's right.' Jessica stared. She didn't know what to say.

'Synchronised swimming. It's like ballet in the water, swimming in formation,' Carrie explained.

'Er, yes. I've seen it on TV. They do it in the Olympics, don't they?' Jessica climbed out to sit on the edge. 'Er, I'm Jessica. I haven't been before. My mum's friend's a member...'

'Have you ever done any synchro?' Anna asked.

'No, but I've done some racin'. Never came first, though.'

'Synchronised swimming isn't about speed,' Carrie explained. 'It's about control and grace. And you've got both. And with some training with the team, who knows where you could go! Will you come and try? We practise here on Tuesday evenings at seven o'clock.'

'Tuesday evenin', that's when— er, yes! I'd love

to!' What a perfect excuse not to go to the drama club! 'Er, thanks!' she said to Carrie.

'Don't thank me. Thank Anna. She's the talent spotter.'

Jessica grinned at Anna.

'We're called the Dolphins,' Anna added.

'Dolphins?'

'Yep! Because they're the most graceful creatures in the water – very intelligent, and they look after each other – work as a team.'

Jessica thought of the shape of dolphins. Then she considered Anna's description. Graceful, intelligent and good team members.

'You'll like it!' Anna assured her.

'Thanks,' Jessica replied. 'I think I might!'

'What's up with you?' Daleep asked Arun as they washed up the dinner dishes. 'You haven't said a word all week. That must be a record, even for you!'

'Nothing,' Arun lied. In fact, he was worried about Jessica. She'd been off school for two days after her fall at the dress rehearsal. When she'd returned to school the following Monday, he'd expected her to have her arm in a sling, or to be walking with crutches, but she seemed fine. She wasn't even limping.

Since his conversation with her on the day of the flour bag incident, he'd realised she wasn't all fists and a thick skull. He hated all the gossip and fun-poking. He wanted to tell everyone to shut up, but he didn't have the guts.

'Must be girl problems,' Daleep guessed.

'No!' Arun said, rather too quickly.

'Ah-ha!' Daleep grinned. 'So it *is* girl problems. Let me guess. Sasha? She's in your class, isn't she? Or Angie...'

'Gimme a break!' Arun growled.

'So, who else could it be? Ella? No, she's with Phil.'

'How do you know?' Arun asked, amazed.

'Oh, I keep my ear to the ground,' Daleep replied mysteriously. 'How about the musical one? What's her name? Claire? No, you wouldn't stand a chance. How about that big girl, Jessica? The one who can slay three boys at a time with one hand behind her back!'

Arun didn't say anything, but his expression must have given him away because Daleep pounced. 'It *is* her! You wanna be careful, mate. That one barks *and* bites!'

'She doesn't!' Arun objected.

Daleep looked amused. Arun was mad. 'She's, she's...' He wanted to stick up for Jessica without giving away anything of the conversation he'd found so helpful. 'Actually, she's very thoughtful. I share a desk with her in FCT. And she's a good actress. She's got a great voice.'

Daleep still looked amused, but there was no mockery in his eyes now. 'Go on,' he urged, laying down his dish towel.

'Well, it's just that, um...'

'You don't know what to say to her?'

'No! Yes. Well, sort of...' Arun looked at Daleep. He expected a list of clever chat-up lines, but the usual hardness had gone from Daleep's expression. Encouraged, he went on, 'She fell. In a drama rehearsal. It was a bad fall. She's quite, um, heavy. And she had a couple of days off school. Everyone laughed about it. Since she came back, she doesn't seem to talk to anyone, and she's left the drama club.'

'And you want to know if she's OK?'

'Yeah!'

'Well, mate, I can assure you, she's fine!' Daleep grinned and punched Arun gently on the shoulder.

'How do you know?'

'She's in the synchronised swimming team at the Country Club Leisure Complex.'

'Where you're on placement?'

'Yep!'

'Are you sure it's her?'

'She's a bit hard to miss, right?'

Arun grinned and nodded.

'What's more, she's good,' Daleep added. 'Tell you what. Why don't you come with me on Tuesday and watch them? It's mostly just mums that stay and watch, but you could sit in the café and have a Coke or something.'

On Tuesday evening, Daleep got permission to take Arun along to the Country Club. While Daleep went off to supervise the Pulse Centre, Arun bought a fizzy drink and a chocolate bar at the Country Club café and sat at one of the tables beside the pool. There was a group of mums chatting and drinking coffee at the table next to him, and he took refuge behind them. He didn't want to be too obvious.

The girls trooped out of the changing rooms and jumped into the pool, ducking and diving, and generally warming up. They were wearing the same swimsuits, black with a sort of wavy white stripe up the side and white swimming hats. Jessica looked great.

As Arun watched, the coach stepped forward and put the girls through their paces, swimming lengths, using different strokes. Jessica glided through the water with no splash at all.

Then the girls formed a circle, skulling on their backs like the spokes of a wheel, their toes almost touching in the middle. At a signal, they each lifted one leg, perfectly straight, pointing their feet at the ceiling, still in circular formation. Then they did backward somersaults, absolutely coordinated, surfacing holding hands, arms outstretched.

Arun forgot about hiding. He craned his neck to get a better view. The display was amazing. He didn't know how these girls could do it, all together, with hardly a ripple in the water. Jessica was stunning. In the water, she didn't look at all large and ungainly. In fact, she had a good, curvy figure. The water shone and glistened on her skin. And she was such a fantastic swimmer – elegant and graceful. She made everything look easy.

Wanting to encourage her, as she had encouraged him, Arun thought about what to say. He'd tell her she was ace. A great swimmer. A winner. So, at the end of the session, when some of the mums stepped forward to hand towels to their daughters and say well done, Arun stepped forward, too.

Jessica obviously hadn't spotted him earlier. 'Hey, Arun! What're you doin' here?'

'Just came to watch,' he grinned. 'Jess, you were,

um, I just thought, er, you're beautiful!' He gasped. That wasn't what he'd planned to say.

Jessica looked stunned for a moment, then she smiled broadly, tugged off her white swimming hat, and shook drops of water from her crinkly hair all over Arun. Laughing, she pranced off to the changing room, but just before she went in, she turned back to look at him. She was still smiling, and she mouthed 'thanks' before she disappeared inside.

Don't hang up

It all started the day Holly's mum died. Gemma went to call for Holly as usual to walk to the Resolution Club. She lived in the next street to Gemma. The curtains were closed even though it was June and the sun was shining, and the house seemed spookily quiet.

It took ages for anyone to answer the door. Finally Holly's brother, Martin, came. 'He said, 'Hi, Gemma. Holly can't come today...' and he told Gemma about their mother's accident. Gemma was so appalled, she didn't know what to say, so she just stuttered that she was very sorry. She didn't see Holly.

The whole thing seemed so unreal. When Gemma arrived at Resolution, everyone was making a racket and larking around as usual, even Bonnie. Eventually, she asked Gemma, 'Where's Holly?' Gemma burst into tears, and everyone fell silent. They all prayed for Holly there and then, and Bonnie said she'd probably have a week or two off school, but that everyone was to be a good friend to her.

The funny thing was, Holly was at school as usual on Monday morning. Gemma said how sorry she was, and Holly said yes, well...

So *I* cried when Holly's mum died, and *Holly* didn't, thought Gemma. Or at least, not while Gemma was around. But after that, they became much closer friends. Holly sort of latched on to Gemma. It might have been because they lived near to each other. Or it might have been because of Gemma's dad. Of course, their situations weren't the same at all because Gemma's dad had left her mum and her when she was very small. Gemma thought he was still alive somewhere, though she never saw him, and she didn't really remember him. Her mum said he might have gone back to Japan where he came from. But it meant both Holly and Gemma had only one parent. Holly seemed to be comfortable in Gemma's house. Or it might have been because Gemma's mum tended to mother her a bit.

Anyway, Gemma told Holly she'd call for her as usual on the Friday evening for Resolution, but she said she couldn't come because they were going to her gran's for tea. Gemma prayed she'd come the next time, but the following week she didn't want to come because she said she couldn't stand everyone being slushy. So Gemma prayed that everyone *wouldn't* be slushy, and she warned them not to be. But the week after that the summer holidays began.

Gemma had to admit it was always fun going around with Holly, especially at the beginning. The teachers let her get away with all sorts of things because of her mum's accident. One morning, Holly was late. Gemma had called round for her, but she'd told Gemma to go on ahead. She said she'd catch her up.

The first period was FCT. They were all just filling in a sheet about a balanced diet when Holly burst in and apologised to Mrs Elliot. Usually they got a detention if they were late without a note, but Mrs Elliot was being soft, because of Holly's mum. Then Holly pulled a little foil parcel out of her bag and unwrapped it. There were two slices of toast with butter and marmalade, and Holly just began to eat them. Gemma could tell Mrs Elliot didn't know what to say. So Holly smiled, and said with her mouth full, 'My dad says everyone should eat breakfast, Miss. It's good for the concentration.' Then Karen Webber began to giggle, and soon they were all laughing hysterically. Even Mrs Elliot smiled.

Everyone could tell the teacher was in a good mood, so Karen said, 'I didn't have any breakfast, Miss. And I'm finding it quite hard to concentrate.' So they all ended up making toast, and Mrs Elliot said they could finish filling in the sheets during the next lesson.

There was another time when Holly, Claire and Gemma went into the library. It was a very warm day, and Miss Black, the librarian, was looking hot and flustered. Holly went straight up to the desk and said loudly, 'Fish, chips and mushy peas, please.'

'Holly Southam! This is a *library*!' Miss Black said, shocked.

'Oh, sorry,' Holly said. She turned round to make sure everyone was looking, then she repeated in a loud stage whisper, 'Fish, chips and mushy peas, please.' The whole place fell about laughing, but Claire and Gemma marched Holly out before Miss Black had time not to take it as a joke. Gemma was concerned about Holly and prayed that she wouldn't get into *real* trouble.

During the summer holidays it was Martin's eighteenth birthday. Holly talked about it a lot. She was always proud of having such a gorgeous big brother. She really liked him. So did everyone. He was cool, and nice with it. Their dad had given Martin some money to go into town with his friends in the evening, but his gran wanted him to have a tea party at home. Martin agreed, just to keep his gran happy, and they invited their aunt and uncle and their baby cousin and Martin's girlfriend. And Martin told Holly to invite a friend, too, so she invited Gemma.

Holly's gran had made a fantastic racing car birthday cake. It must have taken her ages. Holly told her it was silly. She said that only little kids had theme cakes, but Martin went over to his gran and gave her a huge hug and a kiss, and said it was the best cake he'd ever had. Then there was an awkward moment because their mum used to make good birthday cakes, too. But then Mr Southam took photos and Martin opened some presents, and everyone was in a party mood again.

Then the door bell went, and it was Martin's school friend, Robbie. His name was Robert, really, but he liked everyone to call him Robbie, after Robbie Williams. He used to sing in a band at school. He thought he was brilliant, but no one else did. Martin's gran invited him to join the party. He made some pathetic comments about jelly and ice cream and pass-the-parcel, but Gran and Holly's dad had started to clear up by then, and the aunt and uncle said they had to go because it was the baby's bedtime.

Robbie came in and ate cake and drank Coke, and burped like a ten-year-old. Then he began to make comments about how Gemma had grown up, and how it would suit her if she wore her shirt with one or two buttons undone at the top. He kind of leered at her, and made her feel creepy. So she said it was time she went, and thanked them for having her. She stuck her head around the kitchen door to thank Holly's gran who was washing up, and missing Holly's mum so much that tears were dripping off her chin into the dish water. Feeling awkward, Gemma thanked her and said how sorry she was about Holly's mum. Holly's gran dried her hands on her apron, sniffed and smiled, and gave Gemma a big hug.

When Gemma went back through the hall towards the front door, Robbie was trying to grab a can of instant whipped cream from Holly. She had squirted some on his new shirt. Gemma prayed that the two of them wouldn't spoil Martin's birthday.

When September came and the Resolution Club started up again after the school holidays, Gemma prayed hard that Holly would come back. At the end of school on the Friday, Gemma said to her, 'See you later. I'll come round at seven-fifteen as usual.'

'Don't bother,' Holly replied shortly. 'I'm not coming.'

'Why not?' Gemma asked.

'Don't want to. Can't be bothered.'

But Gemma prayed she would change her mind, so she went round anyway, just in case. Holly answered the door, wearing a towelling bath robe. 'I told you, I'm not coming,' she insisted. 'I've just had a shower.'

'I'll wait while you put some clothes on,' Gemma offered.

'Look, Gemma,' she said, putting on that 'I'm-trying-to-be-patient' voice, 'I don't fit in at Resolution any more. You lot, you're all... all trying to... grow your faith, or whatever. But look at me. I haven't got any faith!'

'Don't say that, Holly,' Gemma began. 'God still loves you, even though...'

'How can you believe that!' Holly snapped. 'How could God, if there is a God... how could he love me, or anyone, and let things happen, like how could he let your dad walk out and my mum get killed, and loads of people die in wars and earthquakes... you can keep it!' And she closed the door.

Gemma stood there, staring at her front door for a moment. Then she went on alone to Resolution, praying all the way that God would show Holly he still loved her. Somehow.

The first week Bonnie asked, 'On your own again, Gemma?' Gemma just nodded.

The following weeks Bonnie always said, 'Keep on praying for Holly, Gemma. God's phone is always switched on. Don't hang up.'

All summer they'd been looking forward to the Trenches Trip. It wasn't going to be a holiday. They'd had that drilled into them at school. It was part of the history syllabus, visiting the First World War battlefields in Belgium and northern France, seeing the memorials and graveyards, and walking in a real trench which had been preserved ever since 1918. Even though it wasn't a holiday, they were all still excited because it was a week away, and Karen and Claire had never even been abroad before.

But right from the beginning, they could tell that Holly was going to make trouble. Mr Nevis said they could wander around the ferry as long as they stayed in threes. The trouble started when Holly, Karen and Gemma went to the buffet to buy burgers and chips. A group of boys sitting together at a table stared as they were passing. It was obvious they were German from the badges on their rucksacks.

'Guck mal!' Holly said in a squeaky voice, making it sound like a hiccup. *Guck mal!* was the name of their German language textbook.

'Deutsch? Du sprichst Deutsch? Sehr gut! Komm mal her! Ich heisse Jorg!' said a beefy blond boy, opening his arms in welcome, and patting his knee for Holly to sit down.

Karen and Gemma started to walk on, ignoring them, but they stopped in their tracks when Holly took up the offer. She actually went and sat on the boy's knee! Karen and Gemma hung back, and hissed at her to go and join the food queue. But she wouldn't. She sat on his lap with one arm around his shoulder and came out with all the German phrases she could remember. 'Wie heisst du? Wie alt bist du? Wo wohnst du?' Jorg introduced the others as Klaus, Peter and Stefan. When she had asked them as much as she could about their names, ages and home town, she started nicking chips and bits of sausage off their plates, and took a swig from Stefan's glass. 'Eine gute Bier!' she exclaimed, though Gemma felt sure it was fruit juice.

'Ein gutes Bier,' Klaus corrected her. 'Bier is neuter. You have to make ze adjectives agree.' His accent was strong but his English was brilliant. He could even explain German grammar in English!

'So where are you lot going, then?' Holly asked.

'Home. Ve are going home,' Stefan replied. 'Ve have been to see London. Ve have seen ze Buckingham Palace, ze Science Museum, ve have been to ze shopping in Harrod's...' Their English is so much better than my German, thought Gemma.

'And you?' Jorg asked. 'Where do you go?'

'We're going to see the war graves,' Holly answered. 'And the trenches. We're going to honour the brave British soldiers who were killed by *your* lot.'

'Holly!' Karen and Gemma whispered urgently, 'Leave it. Come on.'

'But ze wars were a long time ago,' Jorg said affably. 'We can all be friends now.' He put both arms around Holly.

'You wouldn't say that if *your* great-grandad was killed in the trenches, or your grandad was killed by the Nazis!' Holly retorted, jumping up. Gemma took hold of her sleeve to try to pull her away, but Holly shrugged her off.

'Ze Nazis divided our country,' Klaus said very seriously. 'We do not support zem.'

'Oh yes!' Holly sneered, 'It's easy enough to say that now, since you *lost* and we *won*!'

Klaus leapt to his feet angrily, and gripped Holly by both shoulders. He started to say something, but Holly began to fight like a cat, clawing, kicking and yelling, until Mr Nevis came striding across the cafeteria, and at the same time a tall, well-dressed German teacher came to join the boys. Immediately, Holly and the boys separated and became silent. 'I'm very sorry,' said the German teacher with a perfect accent, 'if my students have been causing a problem for your student...'

'Mr Nevis, it wasn't their fault!' Karen whispered urgently into her teacher's ear. The two adults looked confused.

'I think it was a misunderstanding,' Mr Nevis said finally, and led Holly, Karen and Gemma away. Gemma's heart was thudding, and Karen was as white as a sheet, but Holly remained silent and sulky. Mr Nevis must have realised it was her fault because he gave Karen and Gemma the right coins and told them to get a cup of hot chocolate out of a drinks machine, and said he was going to talk to Holly.

Gemma put the coin in and watched the soothing warm drink trickle into her cup. Coin in, drink out. Simple. If God is so powerful, why doesn't he answer my prayers for Holly like that? Gemma asked herself. Prayer up, answer down. Surely it would be easy for him, she thought.

After that, Holly was subdued, not her usual funny self. But she didn't say sorry, either. Karen and Gemma felt uneasy with her all the time.

At Tyne Cot Cemetery they were all absolutely amazed by the huge graveyards. They seemed to go on for ever, as far as the eye could see.

In Sanctuary Wood they had to wear their wellingtons and wade through the muddy trench, imagining what it would have been like to live there for weeks at a time.

At Thiepval they looked at all the thousands of names engraved on the war memorial.

'There are over seventy-three thousand names engraved here,' Mr Nevis told them. 'All these men died in the Battle of the Somme. Most of them have no known graves.'

Lots of people looked up their own names, or their mums' maiden names, or the names of any relatives they could think of. One girl even found her great-grandfather's name. While everyone was crowding round to have a look, Gemma saw Holly writing on the marble memorial. 'H Southam,' she wrote, at the right place in the alphabet.

'Holly! You can't write graffiti here!' said Gemma, shocked. She thought Holly was going to write something like 'H Southam woz 'ere', and the date.

'Don't be silly,' Holly told her. 'It's only felt tip.' She licked her finger and rubbed it off. Gemma breathed a sigh of relief. Later, back at the youth hostel, she told Karen who explained that Holly was probably writing a memorial to her mum. Her name was Heather.

But during the afternoon, it was Karen's turn to be subdued. Gemma said, 'Come on, Karen, look for the Webbers. They might not be anyone you knew, but they must be your distant relatives somewhere along the line.' But Karen shook her head and turned away. Holly and Gemma went over to see what was the matter.

Karen was really upset. 'My real name is spelt with only one B. It's Weber.' She pronounced the W as a V, like the German boys had, and the E as an AY. 'My grandad was from the Black Forest, south Germany. My grandad never met his dad. My great-grandad was killed before my grandad was born. He gave his life for his country, but it was the wrong country. We're the enemy really.' She looked anxiously at Holly.

But Holly put her arm around Karen and said, 'Your great-grandad died fighting for his country, trying to do what he thought was right. He was a hero.'

Gemma could see that Karen was very relieved that Holly wasn't going to make any stupid remarks about her being the enemy. But Karen and Gemma both realised that what Holly was really thinking was that her mum's death wasn't heroic – it was just a senseless waste. Gemma realised then how much Holly still thought about her mum, even though she never said anything. So she prayed that God would really comfort Holly.

In October it was Holly's fourteenth birthday. Ever since Martin's eighteenth, she'd been trying to persuade her dad to let her go into town and have a pizza in a restaurant with some friends. He was like the teachers – being soft on her because of all that had happened. So Holly invited Karen, Claire, Ella and Gemma, and they went to Giuliano's. It was a bit smarter than they were used to. The food was delicious, and very expensive. Holly paid for it all with the money her dad had given her. She had told the others not to take any money. They all tried very hard to behave like perfect adults in such a smart place, but as soon as they got outside they giggled so much that people in the street must have thought they were drunk.

Karen, Claire and Ella got a lift home with Karen's dad because they lived in a different direction from Holly and Gemma who had planned to get the bus. It was easy – just one bus, and their houses were only a couple of minutes walk from the bus stop.

When the other three had gone, Holly said, 'It's not very late yet. Let's just walk down by the river. The lights are always reflected. It's like Christmas.'

Gemma said, 'It's too late. We ought to get the bus straight away. I told my mum I'd…'

'I told my mum…' Holly mocked her in a sing-song voice, and immediately Gemma felt guilty for having a mum who was concerned about her. In fact, for having a mum at all. Holly marched off towards the river, leaving Gemma with nothing to do but follow her. Gemma suddenly felt annoyed. At least Holly'd had two parents for nearly fourteen years. She'd only ever had one, for as long as she could remember. Gemma prayed to herself, Lord, it's not fair.

Holly was right. It *was* beautiful by the river. The water was flowing lazily, and coloured lights from The Mississippi, a paddle-steamer-style floating restaurant, were multiplied by the reflections. Music was playing on board, and every now and then the boats honked, just for effect, like river boats in the fog. But there were some weird-looking characters hanging around, and a group of drunk men waving bottles made rude comments as the girls passed by. Gemma wanted to go back to the nearest bus stop, but she couldn't leave Holly alone.

Soon they came to one of the riverside bars. Inside, it looked warm and bright.

'Hey, Holly! Come in here, gorgeous!' It was Robbie. Gemma shuddered, but Holly sucked up to him as though he were a long-lost brother. Gemma wished it was Martin instead, then she'd have felt safe. Robbie was with three other boys who looked older than him.

'What're you drinking, girls?' one of the boys asked.

Holly mentioned the name of a drink Gemma had never heard of. Gemma said, 'I'm not thirsty, thanks.'

'You can't come in here and not be thirsty!' the boy scolded her. Then he went to the bar and soon came back with two similar glasses for both of them. Gemma looked around, feeling guilty. She was fourteen, not eighteen, and knew she'd never looked old for her age. She thanked the boy anyway, and pretended to sip the drink though she didn't actually swallow any of it. Holly did, though. Robbie brought two chairs for them, and pulled Holly down close to himself. Gemma had to sit wedged between two of the other boys and try to make conversation. Mostly they said things she didn't understand, and then laughed. So she laughed, too, so as not to seem rude.

But inside Gemma was really scared. Holly was leaning on Robbie and laughing a lot. She had already drunk quite a bit of the drink and her cheeks were unnaturally pink. Help, Lord, Gemma prayed silently. Please get us out of here safely.

Suddenly, Robbie stood up and pulled Holly to her feet. 'Time to go, girls,' he said hastily. 'See you again.' And he hustled Holly and Gemma out, leaving them on the walkway beside the river while he went back inside, just as two policemen strolled past.

'Well! That dirty, rotten…' Holly started to follow him back inside, but Gemma pulled her back.

'No, Holly. We're too young, and we've got to get the bus home.'

The next event happened so quickly, it was all over before they could blink. There was a shout, and a big splash. They ran to the rail to look into the river, and as they did so, they got separated for a moment by a group of rowdy young people, not much older than them, and mostly boys. The boys jostled them and pushed them, and Gemma was afraid for a moment they were trying to tip them into the water. Then the boys ran off, and it was over as soon as it had started. Gemma got hold of Holly's arm and began to pull her away from the river, back to the bus stop.

Suddenly, Holly stopped and yelled, 'My bag! My bag's gone!' They looked around wildly, helplessly.

'It must have been that gang that bumped into us,' Gemma suggested. But they were long gone, and the only people they could see didn't look like the types who might help them. Then a terrible thought struck Gemma. 'Holly, I don't have enough bus fare to get us both home. You promised to pay. You said this evening was on you.'

'Just check,' Holly pleaded, reasonable for a moment. 'You might have more than you thought.' They opened Gemma's bag, and there wasn't enough. But she had her mobile phone.

'Let's phone your dad, or my mum,' she suggested. 'They'll come and fetch us.'

'No!' Holly pleaded. 'I'll get into terrible trouble.'
Then she took Gemma's phone and ran off with it,
along the river walkway.

Gemma was really mad with her now. She ran to
catch up with Holly and tried to make a grab for the
phone. Holly twisted out of her reach. She was
looking through the list of numbers stored on the
phone. She began dialling one. Gemma breathed a
sigh of relief and began to relax. She was phoning
home after all. But she started to giggle silently, and
cleared her throat. She held the phone where they
could both listen. Gemma heard a familiar voice
answer. It was Bonnie.

'Hello, Bonnie,' Holly growled in a low voice.
'This is Jesus. I thought it was time we had a little
chat.'

Gemma gasped, horrified. She pictured her phone
number displayed on Bonnie's phone, and couldn't
imagine what Bonnie was thinking. There was a split
second's pause, then the friendly, familiar voice came
back, 'Hello, Lord. I'm so glad to hear from you.
There are so many things I wanted to chat with you
about. For a start, there's Holly Southam. Please
would you remind her how much you love her. Tell
her that her mother is safely with *you* now. Help her
to realise how many friends she's got who really want
the best for her. And don't let her forget that you
died in order to forgive her...' Holly's shoulders
began to shake, and for an awful moment Gemma
thought she was giggling. Then she handed the phone
to Gemma who could see she was sobbing. Tears
were gushing down her cheeks. She seemed to go
limp, and sat down suddenly in the middle of the

walkway. Gemma had never seen anything like it. She felt shaky. Her knees were wobbling so much she thought she was going to fall over.

'Gemma, is that you? Don't worry, I'm on my way.'

'On your way?' Gemma repeated stupidly.

'Yes. You're beside the river, aren't you?'

'H-how…?'

'I could hear The Mississippi. I was just driving home along North Bank Street when the phone rang, so I'll be there in just a minute. Come up and stand on the pavement, so I can see you clearly, can you?'

'OK,' Gemma gasped. 'Thank you…' She switched off the phone. 'Come on, Holly. We're getting a lift.'

Gemma hauled Holly to her feet, and for once she didn't resist. They made it to the pavement just in time to see the welcome red car pull up beside them. 'Well done, Gemma,' Bonnie said, getting out of the car to help Holly into the back. Smelling Holly's breath, she wrinkled her nose. 'I think we could probably all do with some coffee at my house before I take you home,' she said. 'Gemma, please phone your mum and her dad, and tell them I'll have you home in three quarters of an hour.'

So Gemma made the phone calls, and then thankfully watched the dark street go by as they drove homewards. Holly hadn't stopped sobbing, but somehow the hardness had gone and Gemma knew she had turned a corner.

'Bonnie?' asked Gemma.

'Uh-huh?' said Bonnie.

'I didn't hang up,' Gemma went on.

'No, I know you didn't,' Bonnie replied.